Tina's Elusive Enemy

· HILDA STAHL ·

Tina's Elusive Enemy

Tyndale House
Publishers, Inc.
Wheaton, Illinois

Dedicated with love to
Brad, Judy, Bradley, Kim, Larry,
and Paul Bennett

Library of Congress Catalog Card Number 80-53788
ISBN 0-8423-7213-X, paper
Copyright 1981 by Hilda Stahl. All rights reserved.
First printing, April 1981
Printed in the United States of America

• CONTENTS •

• ONE •

The Threats

Tina's heart raced in fear as she reread the note printed in bold, black letters on a torn piece of paper. Perspiration stood out on her forehead as she read in a whisper, "I hate you. I'll get you for what you did to me." Who hated her so much?

Her eyes blurred and the words ran together. Who would write a note to her and leave it tucked under her saddle? It had to be someone who knew her daily routine, who watched her every move. Tina's legs gave way and she dropped to a bale of hay. Blaze nickered from his stall. A gray cat rubbed against her leg.

"Who's doing this to me?" she whispered hoarsely. She shivered as she remembered the words in the first note: *You'll be sorry!* She had laughed and stuffed it into her jeans pocket. The second note hadn't made her laugh. *I'm watching you and waiting for the right time.*

"Who's writing these notes to me?" She rubbed her name printed on the note. Whoever had written it knew she was the only Tina on the ranch or he would've written her full name, Tina Lambert.

Nervously she looked around the barn. Was someone watching her right at this minute? Did the person know how scared she felt? She swallowed hard. Maybe she should show the notes to Dad. She shook her head until her long brown hair whipped across her pale face. No! He was too busy with Mary, always kissing her and hugging her and acting happy to have her as his wife.

"Phil! I'll show this to Phil!" Tina clutched the note and stood up slowly. She pushed her plaid shirt down into her jeans as she stumbled from the barn. Phil would help her! Why hadn't she thought of asking him about the notes before? Color flooded back into her suntanned face and the fear inside subsided.

Dust puffed onto her boots and the bottoms of her jeans as she ran across the yard to the corral where Phil would be working with a horse. She squinted against the hot August sun. Phil would know what to do. He always did.

A car rattled past on the road in front of the ranch buildings. Tina shivered as she watched it out of sight. Maybe the driver of the car had left the notes. Once she talked to Phil, she'd be all right.

Tina stopped short. Phil stood beside the fence, talking and laughing with Bridget Hawksley. Tina frowned as she stuffed the note into her pocket. Every time she turned around Phil and Bridget were together. Dad shouldn't have hired a horse trainer with a daughter, especially a daughter almost fifteen, with an eye on Phil. Too bad she wasn't short and fat and ugly instead of tall and slender and attractive.

Tina lifted her rounded chin. At least she was much prettier than Bridget. Everyone told her she could easily pass for sixteen. And Phil didn't mind that she was thirteen.

Phil turned and saw her and she walked toward him as if Bridget wasn't there.

"Hi, Tina," said Phil, with a smile. "I thought you were riding. Did you decide it was too hot today?"

Bridget glared at Tina. "If you think Phil's going with you, just forget it. We made plans and not even the boss's spoiled darling can change them."

Tina lunged for Bridget but Phil caught her around the waist and held her back. She kicked and screamed but he was too strong for her. Bridget's laughter made her angrier still. Oh, when she got free she'd make both of them pay!

"Simmer down, Tina." Phil talked to her as if she was a high-strung filly he was calming down. She forced herself to stay still in his arms and then jerked free as he loosened his hold.

"I'm going to tell Dad to fire your father, Bridget Hawksley!" Tina's eyes flashed with rage as she stared up at the tall red-headed girl.

"Tina. Tina," said Phil, shaking his head. "You and Bridget don't have to fight every time you get close to each other." He reached for her hand but she jumped back. "What's got into you, Tina? You know Steve doesn't want you fighting."

Tina balled her fists at her sides. "And you'd love to tell Dad on me, wouldn't you, Phil? It would make you feel so good!" She narrowed her eyes. "You want to make it big with him so you can be sure to have a home here with your uncle until after high school, maybe even after college."

She saw a muscle jump in his jaw and she knew he was angry. "You're going to be sorry in a little while, Tina," he said in a soft, gentle voice. "You always talk first and then have to apologize later."

"I can't believe the poor little rich girl ever says she's sorry," said Bridget with a sneer.

Tina moved toward her again but Phil caught her again in an iron grip. She was forced to stand still, anger seething inside.

"Stop tormenting Tina, Bridget," said Phil sharply.

Tina stood perfectly still, her eyes wide in surprise.

"You don't know Tina at all. She's a nice girl. Usually." Phil backed against the fence with Tina held against him.

"How can you be fooled by her?" cried Bridget, her hands on her hips. "She's trouble for both of us."

Tina's eyes widened and her heart beat loud enough for Phil to hear it. Was Bridget writing the notes? Did Bridget hate her that much?

"I happen to like Tina," said Phil stiffly. "We're friends." He dropped his hand and she stepped away from him, her thoughts full of ways to prove that Bridget was writing the threatening notes to her.

"Did you want me for something, Tina?" asked Phil as he pulled his hat down over his blond curls.

She touched the note in her pocket. "Not now. I'll talk to you later." Tina wanted to say that she would talk to Phil when he was alone, but she didn't want any ugly comments from Bridget. It would be too hard not to accuse her of writing the notes, and she wanted positive proof before she made a move. "You both better get back to work and earn the money Dad's paying you." The hurt look on Phil's face made her want to tell him she was sorry, but she would not do it in front of Bridget.

With her head high Tina walked toward the ranch house. Later she would talk to Phil. Fear clutched her stomach. What if he didn't want to talk to her? She had been meaner than usual to him since Bridget came. Was it her fault? She shook her head impatiently. Bridget hadn't liked her from the first day and Tina certainly couldn't be expected to like a girl who continually threw herself at Phil.

A horse nickered. A tractor roared in the hayfield in back of the shed.

Tina forced herself to keep walking and not look back at Phil. Did he still love her? He hadn't kissed her since they'd been fishing together several days ago. Maybe he'd decided she was too young and that Bridget would make a better girl friend. Tears stung Tina's eyes and she blinked fast to keep them from falling. She would not think about Phil right now. She would not cry. She had to find a way to prove that Bridget was writing threatening notes to her. Maybe then Dad would fire Hawk, and if Hawk left, Bridget would have to go, too.

The air-conditioned house felt cool and comfortable and Tina leaned weakly against the closed door, the note in her hand. She heard Mary and Dad talking in the study. She knew they hadn't heard the door close. They never heard anything but each other when they were together.

Slowly Tina walked to her bedroom, reading the note again. Bridget would be very sorry for scaring her! And Phil would realize that Bridget wasn't a girl he'd want to love.

Tina pulled the two other notes from her desk drawer and laid all three notes on her desk. She frowned as she touched the penciled scrawl of the first note. When had she received that note? Was it after Bridget and Hawk moved here? It had to be! What other enemy could she have? Or could this be a practical joke that one of the ranch hands was playing on her?

Slowly Tina sank to her chair and thoughtfully fingered the notes. All three of them were written on a cheap grade of typing paper. Two of the notes were written in ink and one in pencil. She shivered and folded her arms around herself. Was she in real danger? Would it be safe to ride Blaze alone across the pasture away from the ranch buildings? Fear pricked her skin. Yesterday she'd been riding alone most of the afternoon. If someone wanted to harm her, wouldn't they have tried then?

She licked her dry lips with the tip of her tongue. "This is ridiculous! I can't be afraid all the rest of my life over three crazy notes. It must be a practical joke. It has to be!"

She grabbed the notes and wadded them into a tight ball and dropped them into the wastebasket. "That takes care of that!"

With a toss of her long brown hair she

turned away and walked to her window. She would saddle Blaze and ride over to visit Codge. She hadn't seen much of him since she and Phil had stopped Dallas Tromley and his two friends from robbing him.

Tina shook her head and wrinkled her small nose. How could she ever have imagined herself in love with Dallas Tromley? And she had let him kiss her! "Yuk!" She rubbed her mouth, trying to rub the memory away.

She turned and stared at the wastebasket. Slowly she picked out the crumpled notes and smoothed them straight. Had Dallas written them? She pressed her hand to her wildly beating heart. He might have. He had been very angry when she'd stopped him from getting money from Codge Farenholz. She'd seen him in church with his mother last Sunday and he had glared angrily at her and mouthed, "I hate you!"

Would he try to get even?

Fearfully she pushed the notes into her desk drawer and pushed it shut with a bang. "I will find out who's doing this to me! And I'll take care of them but good!"

▪ TWO ▪

Runaway

Phil stood with his hands lightly on his slim hips, his feet apart, a scowl on his face. "I can't figure you out, Tina Lambert. Just a couple of weeks ago you asked the Lord to take charge of your life. Now, here you are trying to run it yourself and doing a miserable job of it!"

Tina stood straight, her back against Blaze's stall. She would not allow Phil to see how much his words hurt her. "I said I'm sorry, Philip Rhyner! What do you want me to do? Crawl on my hands and knees? Eats worms?"

He sighed and shook his head, his blond curls damp against his head where his hat band had pressed. "I want you to grow up a little, Tina. Why do you always say things to hurt me? Why are you always mad at Bridget?"

Tears stung her eyes but she refused to let them fall. She couldn't answer his questions. She didn't know the answers herself. Being a Christian was important to her, but new. How did she know what to do and say and how to act? She wasn't Mary, her stepmother, who seemed to automatically do everything right.

Phil stepped forward, his eyes on her face. "I'm sorry, Tina. I have no business coming down on you so hard." He touched her cheek and she didn't dare move or she'd burst into tears. "You said you wanted to talk to me about something important. What is it? I'll help you all I can."

She opened her mouth to tell him about the notes but Bridget dashed in, her small black cocker spaniel at her heels.

"Daddy wants you right away, Phil. He's having trouble with that new gelding."

Tina wanted to scream as Phil grabbed his hat and rushed away. What had happened to the precious moments she and Phil had shared? Would Bridget always be there to interrupt?

Bridget pushed her red hair away from her face. "Daddy said you could help him too if you want too."

Tina's eyes widened in surprise. Hawk had said she was to stay away from the horses he trained until he learned how competent she was. "What can I do?"

Bridget shrugged and spread her hands. "I reckon Daddy knows what he's doing, but if I were him I wouldn't trust you with anything."

"What does he want me to do?" Tina stepped close to Bridget impatiently. "It must be important or he wouldn't have said anything." Even though she didn't like Bridget, she admired Hawk and his work with horses. He was about the best horse trainer she'd ever seen.

"He tied Charger to the post. He said you could run him if you want to. I told him you were Miss High and Mighty and wouldn't take orders or suggestions from him." She bent down and scooped her dog into her arms. "Let's get out of here, Peanut. We don't want to get yelled at again."

Tina laughed aloud in her excitement as she rushed out of the barn. She would not let Bridget's mean words make her angry now. Hawk was finally going to trust her with an animal he was training. And to think Charger was to be the first!

She could not take her eyes off the beautiful black gelding as she hurried across the yard. Even the saddle on his back was one of Hawk's favorites. He finally trusted her! He knew she was good with horses and he knew she would be good with Charger!

"Howdy, big boy," she said softly as she gently stroked his face. "I am going to ride you. Hawk said I could. You and I will be friends. Won't you like that?" Oh, she would like Dad to see her now. He would be mighty proud.

Tina looked at the garage. Dad and Mary weren't back from town yet. They wouldn't be much longer since it was getting close to supper time. Should she wait to ride Charger when Dad was there to see? Tina shook her head. Hawk might change his mind. She turned to look toward the corral but Hawk and Phil weren't in sight. Bridget stood beside her small house that she shared with her daddy.

"Ready, Charger?" Tina slipped her hat off her back and onto her head. She rubbed her hands down her jeans. "Here goes, big boy." Slowly she grabbed the saddle horn and swung into the large saddle. It would have been better to have her saddle with the stirrups fixed to her leg length.

"Tina!"

She looked over her shoulder as Hawk shouted to her. Why was he angry? Before she could find out Charger leaped into the air and ran across the yard into the open pasture. Tina pulled on the reins but nothing happened. "Whoa, Charger!" she shouted over his pounding hooves. "Steady, boy!" But she knew he wasn't listening and that he wouldn't respond to her commands. He was running away and she couldn't stop him. She was too weak. Once she thought of leaping off, but Charger was running too fast for her to land properly.

Frantically she clutched the saddle horn and leaned down over the big black gelding's neck. Her mouth felt cotton dry with fear. Her throat ached from shouting. Her ears were filled with pounding hooves. Oh, she should not have taken Bridget's word. Hawk had told her often that she could never ride the horses he trained.

Wind tugged at her hat and almost blew it off her head. Suddenly the pounding grew louder and she was afraid her head would explode. Tears stung her eyes. Was it possible for God to help her now? How would she ask for help? Phil wasn't there to tell her, nor Mary.

Suddenly she was jerked almost out of the saddle. She blinked and looked as Hawk, mounted on Colonel, grabbed Charger's bridle and finally stopped him.

The silence rang in Tina's ears and she trembled so much that she almost fell from the horse.

"Are you crazy, Tina Lambert?" Hawk's dark brows almost met over his large nose. His dark eyes were filled with rage. "I told you never to ride one of my horses."

Tina's mouth fell open and she could only stare.

"I know you're the boss's daughter but that don't mean you can do foolhardy things like this. You could ruin a good horse. Don't you care? What's wrong with you?"

"I thought I could ride Charger," she said weakly.

"Don't lie to me, little girl."

Tina stiffened. How dare he! "Dad will hear about this, Hawk! You can't talk to me this way."

"I can and did, little girl. Get off that horse and walk back to the ranch."

"I will not!" Her blue eyes flashed bluer and she tried to break away from Hawk. "I can handle Charger now. He just needed to run. I'll ride back to the ranch."

"Get down." Hawk's voice was low and firm and Tina knew that she had to obey.

Her legs shook as she stood in the tall prairie grass looking up at the angry man. His hat was pushed back on his head and she could see sweat on his face and staining his shirt. "Ask your daughter why I rode Charger, Hawk. Let her tell you a few lies."

"Do you always lay the blame on others? Take what's comin' to you like the spunky kid you are."

She wanted to scream and rant and rave but she stood still as he turned and rode away, leading Charger. Oh, she hated him! She hated everyone, especially Bridget Hawksley.

Tina pressed her hands to her hot cheeks. Was this Bridget's way of getting even? Had Bridget meant for Charger to throw her, maybe injure her seriously? Maybe the threatening notes would stop now that Bridget had done this. Or maybe Bridget wouldn't quit until she lay dead somewhere for a coyote to pick her bones.

▪ THREE ▪
The Spanking

Tina stood in the hot late afternoon sun until the tall, lean man full of anger rode out of her sight. She jerked as a grasshopper landed on her arm, then jumped into the tall prairie grass. She ignored the beautiful warble of a meadow lark.

What was happening to her life? Being a born-again Christian was supposed to make a difference. Mary and Dad had said so; Phil had, too.

With an unhappy sigh Tina pushed her hat off her head onto her slender back. Slowly she walked through the waist-high grass toward the ranch. Maybe she should talk to Mary. She'd been a Christian for a long time and she might have the answers. But maybe Mary would be too engrossed with Dad to give any advice. How long would the honeymoon go on?

A jackrabbit leaped high, then bounded out

of sight toward the pines. A crow cawed. Tina sadly shook her head. Life still went on even though she was in big trouble. What would Dad say? Would he bawl out Hawk or would he punish her? She frowned into the distance. Why hadn't someone ridden out to pick her up? Had Hawk forbidden it as a punishment for her?

"He wouldn't dare! He's not my boss!" Her lips felt cracked and dry and a thought of a tall glass of cold water sounded heavenly. Hawk would pay for leaving her out here to walk back to the ranch! He'd pay for every aching muscle and cracked lip.

She saw Phil first as she walked into the ranch yard. He rushed to her, calling her name in concern.

"How dare you let me walk home, Phil?" She stood with her fists doubled at her sides, her chin in the air. "Why didn't you pick me up? Were you afraid you'd make Bridget's daddy mad?"

"Stop it, Tina!" He tried to catch her arm but she jerked away.

"Did you even care that I had to walk all that way? Did you even once think about me?"

"You're asking for it, Tina Lambert," he said between his teeth.

She stamped her booted foot. "I hate you, Philip Rhyner! I never want to see you or talk to you again!" Why was she yelling at him? He hadn't done anything to her. She bit her tongue to stop the flow of angry words but they kept rushing out of her. She could see Phil was getting as angry as she was.

Finally he lunged at her and grabbed her arms in a grip of steel. "Take that back!"

She was so angry she didn't know what she'd said to him. Frantically she struggled, screaming and yelling to be set free. Her face flamed as she saw the ranch hands, along with Bridget Hawksley, standing beside the barn, watching and listening.

"I'm going to do something your daddy should have done years ago," said Phil gruffly.

Her eyes widened in alarm and she lay perfectly still against him. Did he mean he was going to spank her? He had often threatened to do it. Oh, he couldn't. But what if he did— in front of everyone?

"Don't you touch me," she whispered savagely.

He forced her around and bent her over and she kicked and screamed but he managed to strike her several hard blows that hurt.

"Stop fighting me, Tina. I can do this all day long if I must."

Tears streamed down her dusty face. Oh, she wanted to sink through the ground! How Bridget must be laughing!

"Say you're sorry, Tina." Phil's mouth was close to her ear, his breath warm against her.

She gritted her teeth. She would not say she was sorry!

"Say it, Tina, or I'll spank you again."

She knew he meant it. "I'm sorry," she whispered.

"When I let you go, you get to the house. If you say anything ugly, I'll catch you and do it again."

Oh, he was terrible! How well he knew her! She could smell the sweat and dust on him as he slowly stood her upright. How she wanted to turn on him and sock him in the nose! And she would the first chance she got.

A horse neighed and another answered. Someone coughed. Tina wondered how many of the hands were laughing at her. Had Bridget put Phil up to this?

"Go right to the house, Tina," Phil said softly. "I mean it."

She felt him release her and for one wild minute she thought her legs would refuse to support her. She would die if she collapsed in front of everyone. She squared her shoulders and flipped her hair out of her face. She caught a glimpse of Bridget's pleasure in her distress.

With a wicked grin Tina turned back to Phil. "Thanks. I needed that," she said, loud enough for the others to hear. She saw the surprise on Phil's face. While he was still off balance at her reaction she threw her arms around his neck and kissed him full on the mouth. Then with her head high she walked to the house. Shouts of laughter and calls to

Phil and herself filled her ears. She had to make it to the house before her legs gave way. She would not let fresh tears fall until she was safely in her room away from everyone.

The quiet, cool house brought instant relief. At last she was away from everyone. Phil was left behind, forced to face all of them alone. Had the kiss angered Bridget?

In her room Tina flung herself across her bed and closed her stinging eyes. She trembled, then lay still, her head against her plaid turtle. Phil must never know how humiliated she'd been. She pressed her face tightly into her turtle. How could he spank her in front of everyone? He would pay! Oh, he would pay well for doing such a terrible thing to her!

"Tina! We're home!"

She sat up, brushing quickly at the tears. Dad would take care of Phil! Dad would fire Slim Rhyner, or insist that Slim send Phil away.

"I'm in my room, Dad." She tugged her shirt in place and shoved it into her jeans. "I want to talk to you."

The door opened and Mary walked in with Dad behind her. "What happened to you, Tina?" asked Mary in alarm, her brown eyes wide. "Oh, Steve. We shouldn't have stayed away so long."

"Tina's tough, Mary," said Steve, looking down at Tina with a questioning look on his face. He was dressed in faded jeans and a blue plaid shirt. He looked tall and lean next to Mary.

Tina hesitated. She'd wanted to talk to Dad alone, but she knew he wouldn't make Mary leave. He wanted Mary to be her mother.

"What is it, Tina?" asked Mary, taking her hand and holding it. "Did something happen while we were gone?"

Tina pulled her hand free and flung herself against her dad, her arms around his waist, her head on his broad chest. He would never turn down her request. Finally she looked up at him and he held her away and studied her face, his eyebrow cocked.

"Phil beat me up, Daddy. He really did!"

"Tina. Tina. I know that boy. He likes you too much to hurt you. Let's go in the front room and sit down and you tell me all about it."

Tina shivered. He wasn't going to listen! He would take Phil's side if she wasn't very careful.

"Come, Tina," Mary said firmly as she took Tina's arm and led her into the large front room.

Tina sank to the couch, her eyes on the stone fireplace that covered the end wall.

"Let's hear it," said Steve as he sat across from her in his favorite chair.

Mary held Tina's hand firmly. "Start at the beginning, honey."

Tina took a deep breath, then let it out. The

clock ticked loudly. Steve's chair groaned as he moved. Tina smelled Mary's perfume and it made her think of how Mother smelled. She pushed the thought aside. Right now she had to tell Dad what had happened so he would feel sorry for her and punish Bridget, Hawk, and Phil.

▪ FOUR ▪

Steve
Loves Mary

As she finished her story Tina watched the expression on Dad's face. She knew he was upset. She hid a smile. Someone would be very sorry—and soon! She had left out the part about kissing Phil. Dad might not appreciate that.

The mantel clock chimed six, startling Tina. Why wasn't Dad talking, or better yet leaping up to fight for her cause? Her stomach tightened.

"Tina, I don't want you trying to get even with Phil. From what I read between the lines he was pushed beyond endurance."

Tina leaped up. "What?"

"Sit down!" Steve pointed to the couch dramatically. "Sit down and listen to me, Tina."

Oh, she didn't want to! She wanted to scream at him, ask him what was wrong with him.

"Tina, you must look at this problem from the others' point of view," said Mary gently. "Don't get too wrapped up in yourself that you can't feel what others are feeling."

"This is not your business," Tina said sharply to Mary. "This is between Dad and me."

"Tina!" Steve pushed himself up and towered over her. "I want you to apologize to Mary this minute. This is as much her business as mine. We are a family now." He glared at her until she meekly said she was sorry.

Steve paced from the window to the coffee table, his hands locked behind his back. "I know I've spoiled you since your mother died. I know I raised you without the Lord, but all that is changed now. I want you to be the best person you can be. I will not allow you to run over everyone in your path. And most of all, I will not allow you to talk unkindly to Mary."

Tina forced herself to stand still. She had gone too far again. A band tightened around her heart and squeezed. Once again she was alone against the world. Dad loved Mary. Mary loved Dad. She was outside of everything.

Finally Steve dropped into his chair and told Tina to sit down again. She reluctantly obeyed.

"First off, Tina, I want you to tell Hawk you're sorry for riding Charger. You should have known that you weren't allowed to, even if ten people said you could. Then, you tell Phil you're sorry for talking mean to him."

Tina's head jerked up. How did Dad know she'd talked mean to him? She hadn't told that part of the story.

"I know Slim Rhyner's nephew wouldn't touch you unless you provoked him. He's a gentle boy."

Mary patted Tina's hand. "Remember that you aren't alone, Tina. You have God helping you. He will give you the strength to say you're sorry."

Tina wanted to rub the touch of Mary's hand off hers, but she sat very still and listened with what she hoped was the right facial expression. How could she have thought she loved Mary? Mary was nothing but trouble for her, for the Lambert family.

"I'll call Hawk to the house and then you tell him you're sorry." Steve walked to the phone and dialed Hawk's house.

"Relax, Tina," said Mary softly. "Hawk won't humiliate you. He'll think more of you."

Tina stared down at her hands clasped in her lap. She dare not tell Mary to shut up. Reluctantly she admitted that Mary was being kind and helpful.

"Now that you're a Christian, Tina, you are a new creature. The Bible says that old things have passed away and that all things are become new. In Christ Jesus your old nature is dead. Your new nature is alive."

"Then why do I act this way?" she asked sharply.

"Because your old self doesn't want to die. You have the choice, honey. You always have the choice on how you act."

Tina shook her head. "I can't help myself."

"Yes, you can—with God's strength and help." Mary pushed her dark curls away from her pretty face. "It's very important to learn God's Word so that it will be inside your spirit to help you every minute of your life."

Tina's heart softened. She did want to do what was right. She did want God to help her. She listened as Mary told her Scripture verses to think about right now. When Mary stopped, Steve caught Tina's hand and pulled her up.

"Hawk will be here in a minute. You talk to him in the study alone. When you're done, I'll talk to him."

Tina's legs felt weak but she stood up straight with her chin high. "I'll brush my hair and wash my face first, Dad. I'll be right back."

He nodded thoughtfully and she knew he was wondering what she was up to. She'd show him that she could do something right. She smiled hesitantly then hurried toward the bathroom. Just as she reached the door she heard him say, "Thank you, Mary. Between us we'll make her into a wonderful kid."

Tina leaned against the closed bathroom

door, her heart racing. She thought Dad had liked her just the way she was. Hadn't he taught her to stand up and fight against all odds?

Quickly she splashed cold water on her face and rubbed it dry with a soft yellow towel. Tears stung her eyes as she pulled a brush through her tangled hair. She jumped as someone knocked on the door and Mary told her that Hawk was waiting for her in the study.

"This is it," she whispered. She moistened her lips with the tip of her tongue as she opened the bathroom door.

"Relax, Tina," Mary said with a smile.

"I'm trying to."

"Would you like me to pray with you?"

Tina hesitated. Someday she'd have to learn to pray on her own, but right now Mary's offer was too good to pass up. She nodded and bowed her head as Mary prayed. The tension inside melted away and Tina was able to smile and say thank you.

In the study she closed the door and looked up at the tall, lean man. He held his hat in his large, sun-blackened hands. His dark hair hung on his wide forehead. He stood quietly, waiting, watching.

"Hawk, I'm sorry for riding Charger. I'm sorry for being rude to you." She watched a smile spread across his face as she held out her hand. His large hand enveloped hers.

"I'm mighty sorry, too, little girl. I don't think you hurt Charger. And you sure did stick on his back like a burr."

Tina grinned. "I've been riding all my life."

"I reckon I can believe it now. It'd be better to stick with a mount that's not too strong for you."

"I know, Hawk."

"I'm sorry about the spanking."

Her face flamed and she looked down at the tips of his boots.

"I didn't mean to embarrass you. That kiss you gave Phil made up for what he did to you. The guys have been teasing him bad."

She wanted to ask if the kiss had made Bridget angry but she didn't. She talked a few minutes more, then told him to wait to talk to her dad. "Don't worry about him firing you, Hawk. You're the best horse trainer we ever had."

"You got the best horses I ever worked with. I sure want to stay as long as I can."

Tina smiled and opened the door just as Steve was ready to knock. He looked from Tina to Hawk, then smiled. He said he could see things were settled and that he'd only keep Hawk a few minutes.

Tina walked slowly back to her room. It had felt good to apologize. Maybe it wouldn't be hard to apologize to Phil. She grinned. And she *had* gotten even with him.

Mary poked her head in the door and held

out an envelope. "I found this in the pickup, Tina. I don't know who put it there."

Tina reached for it, then gasped. Was it another threatening note?

"What's wrong, Tina? Why does a letter frighten you?"

Tina cleared her throat. "No reason." She took the letter and Mary walked away. Soft music from the kitchen radio drifted into Tina's room.

She shivered and the letter crackled in her hands. The room seemed to spin, then stand still. Finally she tore open the envelope and pulled out the note. She dropped in relief to her chair beside her desk. It was only a contemporary greeting card. The outside of the card was covered with flowers and said, "TO THE MOST BEAUTIFUL GIRL IN MY WORLD." She opened it with a surprised smile, then gasped. "I love you" was crossed out and "I hate you" was printed in bold, black ink in its place. It was signed, "Your Executioner."

"Oh! Oh!" Tina dropped the card and stared at it in horror. What could she do?

"I'll show Dad," she whispered as she frantically grabbed the other notes from the drawer. The chair almost tipped over in her haste.

Finally she found him in the kitchen, but his arms were around Mary and he was too engrossed in her to notice anyone else.

Slowly Tina walked back to her room and

pushed the notes into her desk drawer. Shivers ran up and down her spine and she clung to the back of the chair, her eyes wide with terror. She had to fight this alone. No one cared enough for her to help her. Maybe tonight she'd be murdered in her bed!

FIVE

An Old Boyfriend

Impatiently Tina looked around the empty classroom. She saw two Bibles, one under a chair and one on a table, but neither was hers. Where had she left hers? Her soft yellow dress brushed against her legs as she walked around the chairs. Yellow barrettes held her brown hair out of her face. Dad and Mary would be waiting for her if she didn't hurry. With her hands on her slender waist she looked around the room.

"Lose something, Tina?"

She spun around, her heart racing as she looked up at Dallas Tromley. The look in his brown eyes frightened her, but she stood her ground and actually managed a smile. "My Bible. But I can find it later. Dad's waiting for me." She started past him but he caught her wrist in a tight grip and she forced back a gasp. She would not let him see that he upset her in the least.

"It wasn't long ago that you couldn't wait

to be with me," he said gruffly. "Remember our picnic on Tanner Hill? I should take you back there to finish what we started."

"Let me go, Dallas. You're hurting me." She watched a wicked smile spread across his handsome face and his grip tightened until she winced with pain. "Cut it out, Dallas! Do you want me to scream for Dad?"

Dallas laughed, his dark head thrown back. "He wouldn't hear you. He's busy talking with friends in front of the church. Mary's right beside him where she belongs."

Tina shrugged. "Is that supposed to bother me? I'm glad Dad and Mary are married. They're happy together."

"Uh huh. I can believe you're glad. I can believe that you never have a jealous moment." He leaned down to her, his breath hot on her face and she tried to pull away. "I know what a jealous cat you can be." He caught her other wrist and locked them behind her back, bringing her up against him in a way that once would have thrilled her.

"Stop struggling, you little spitfire," said Dallas gruffly. "I have something to say to you, and I mean to say it now."

She wanted to kick and fight and scream, but she managed to stand perfectly still and he pulled away just a little so that they weren't touching.

"You caused me and my buddies a lot of trouble. Larry and Carl left town, but I can't.

Ma needs me here and I'll stay until she's able to take care of herself." A muscle jumped in his jaw. "You owe me something, Tina. You made me lose all that money from old man Farenholz. I'll find a way to make you pay me back."

"You're crazy. Do you think Dad will give me money so I can give it to you?" Her blue eyes flashed and she made the mistake of trying to pull free. His grip tightened and she moaned with pain, biting her lip to keep back a yell. He could easily break her arms if she cried out, and by the looks of him, he wouldn't hesitate to do just that.

"You think that's the only way for me to take revenge?" He chuckled dryly. "Grow up, little girl."

"Leave me alone, Dallas Tromley." She would not let him see how his words and his tone frightened her. She pushed away the ugly thoughts that tried to enter her mind. "You'll be sorry for holding me this way. You'll be sorry for every word you've said to me."

"What a little tiger! You almost scare me." He dropped her wrists but stood against the door so that she couldn't leave.

"Dad's waiting for me, Dallas." She rubbed her red wrists and tried to slow her wildly beating heart.

"I know you and that old man are good friends." She knew he was talking about Codge Farenholz. "I want you to tell him that

I've reformed, that I'd be a good one to work for him."

She rolled her eyes. "And he'd believe me, wouldn't he?"

Dallas stepped toward her and she had to force herself to stand still. "He believes everything you tell him. You're special to him. Even a blind man can see that."

"Forget it! It would be the biggest lie in the world if I told him you'd be a good worker for him."

Dallas's face darkened with rage. "Are you too good to lie now that you've got religion? Is all this church stuff that you used to hate so much changing you into some kind of saint?"

She wanted to say that it was, but she couldn't see much difference in herself, so she kept her mouth tightly closed. Somehow she had to get out of the room away from Dallas.

"You talk to Codge Farenholz, Tina. You tell him to hire me. I need the money. Ma needs the money. You *owe* me something."

She cradled her arms tightly against herself to stop from shivering. "I don't owe you anything. You were wrong to try to steal Codge's money. You brought the trouble on yourself."

He raked his fingers through his dark hair. "Tina, I need money now! Help me, will you?"

For just an instant her heart softened, then she shook her head. "I can't. I don't trust you. Maybe I never will."

He knotted his fists at his sides and leaned forward, his face close to hers. "You will be sorry! When I find you alone, you'll pay for everything you've done to me."

She thought of the notes and trembled. Had Dallas written them? Was he more desperate to get even than she'd thought?

Steps sounded in the hall outside the room and Dallas turned quickly, much to Tina's relief. She caught the back of a chair and held on as he walked from the room. She heard the voices but her head seemed to be spinning away from her and she couldn't catch the words.

"Did he hurt you, Tina?"

"Oh, Phil!" She had forgotten that she had said she'd never speak to him again after she'd been forced to apologize two days before. The sight of him in his blue cords and white shirt and his gentle manner sent her flying into his arms.

"What's this?" he asked as he held her until finally she stopped shaking enough to stand on her own.

With a deep breath she stepped away from him and smiled. "He scared me, that's all."

Phil's hazel eyes narrowed. "It must have been some scare for you to admit it. Will you tell me about it?"

"I . . . I can't right now. Dad's probably looking for me."

"He is. He sent me for you. He said to tell

you that Mary has your Bible. She said it turned up with her things somehow." He reached out to her and she laid her hand in his. "You'll tell me later today, won't you?"

She nodded, wishing she could stand with him like this forever.

"We'll take a ride together so we can be alone."

She knew he meant away from Bridget and she nodded thankfully. "I have a lot to tell you." Today she'd show him the notes and ask him to help her.

"Tina?"

She saw the hesitation in his eyes. "What?"

"Do you still like Dallas?"

She shook her head. Didn't Phil know she loved *him?* But how could he? She'd told him often lately that she hated him. At times she'd thought she had. "Do you like Bridget?" She wanted to ask if he liked Bridget better than her but she was afraid of what he would answer. He would not lie to save her feelings.

He shrugged. "She's all right."

Tina smiled and he smiled back and the world seemed to stand still.

"Your parents are waiting, Tina," Phil said softly as he tugged her toward the door. "We'll talk this afternoon."

"I can't wait!" Phil would help her deal with the notes and with Dallas. But what if Bridget were writing the notes? Would he help put a stop to it then?

Abruptly Tina stopped and Phil turned to her with his eyebrows raised questioningly. "Promise you won't let Bridget tag along today."

He squeezed her hand. "I won't let her. I promise."

"If you learned she was doing something really bad, would you stop liking her?"

He laughed. "Tina, I don't stop liking you when you do something really bad."

She wrinkled her nose at him. "You weren't supposed to say that." She had to be content as she walked with him into the bright sunlight.

SIX

Another Note

Mary looked up from peeling a cucumber for the salad. "Tina, what were you and Phil talking about so earnestly when you walked from the church?"

Tina gripped the carrot tighter and kept her eyes on the peeler in her hand. "Nothing much."

"I know something has been bothering you the past few days, Tina. I'll help you in any way that I can."

Soft music drifted through the kitchen from the radio on the counter. Roast beef and escalloped potatoes filled the room with delicious aromas.

Finally Tina looked up at Mary. "I don't want to talk about it." Didn't Mary know this was none of her business? The hurt look on Mary's face made her feel bad, but she would not give in and talk about her problems.

"I am here when you need me, Tina. You can trust me."

Methodically Tina peeled three carrots. Dare she trust Mary? Would she be able to help find the person writing the threatening notes and stop him? Could Mary keep Dallas from causing trouble for her? She knew other girls who said they talked to their mothers all the time. If Mother were still alive, would she talk to her?

Suddenly she was reliving the pain and agony of hearing that Mother had been killed in a flash flood and would never come home to her again.

"Tina, what's wrong?" asked Mary in concern. "You're as white as this plate."

Tina sagged against the counter, drawing in great breaths of air. She would not think of Mother. The pain was too great. She had thought it was buried deep inside and forgotten.

Strong arms pulled her close and she looked up as Steve drew her against his broad chest.

"Whatever is bothering you can be shared with us, honey. With us and the Lord to help you, no problem is too big to handle." He rubbed his cheek against the top of her head. "Talk to me, little girl. Tell your old dad what's bothering you."

She pressed tighter against him, her eyes closed. He smelled like the outdoors and pine aftershave lotion. She knew he and Mary were exchanging questioning glances. Finally she pushed away and forced a wide smile.

"I'm hungry, Dad. I didn't eat much break-fast this morning. Mary worries over every little thing."

"Have it your way, Tina," Steve said softly, his palm against her cheek. "But you aren't fooling me or Mary. When you're ready to talk, we'll be here."

But she knew he would get engrossed in Mary again and forget he'd even offered his help. It just wasn't like it had been before he married Mary. "Do you think we can eat now? I'm starved." Could she swallow anything?

She found that she could eat enough to keep Dad or Mary from asking about the loss of appetite.

Just as she helped Mary finish loading the dishwasher, Mary said, "Oh, Tina. I left our Bibles and my purse in the car. Will you please run out and get them? Mrs. Lewis gave me a recipe for a dessert I think Steve will like, and I want to make it this afternoon."

The thought of her Bible made her think again of Dallas and his threats. Oh, it would be good to talk to Phil and share her problems with him!

Bridget's little dog barked and ran to meet Tina as she hurried to the car outside the garage. Tina looked around quickly. Usually Bridget was close by if Peanut was. No one was in sight. The silence seemed unusual.

Heat rushed out at her from inside the car.

She gathered up the Bibles and Mary's purse and walked slowly back to the house. Was Phil done eating yet? Would he be in the barn saddling a horse by the time she slipped into jeans and came back out?

As she handed Mary's things to her, Tina's Bible slipped and she grabbed for it. She caught it but a paper from inside it fluttered to the floor. Tina stared in fear as Mary bent to pick it up.

"Give it to me!" cried Tina, grabbing it from Mary.

"I wasn't going to read it." Mary's cheeks were flushed red and tears stood in her eyes.

"You'd better not!" Tina clutched the note and her Bible to her and ran to her room. With fumbling fingers she locked her door then dropped the Bible to her desk. She unfolded the paper awkwardly. *Meet me Wednesday at the pines or you'll be sorry!*

"Who's *doing* this to me?" she whispered in agony as she pressed her hands down on her desk. It had to be Dallas. No. It could be Bridget. Or a stranger!

Frantically she pulled on her jeans, then stuffed the notes into her pockets. Phil would help her.

Why would she be sorry if she didn't meet her enemy at the pines? She'd be stupid to do it. But maybe she and Phil could go together and end this nightmare once and for all.

Quickly she brushed her hair and tied it in

two ponytails over her ears. She tugged her light blue tee shirt over her jeans and walked to the door.

"Where're you going, Tina?" asked Steve as he looked up from the book he was reading.

"Out riding with Phil. We'll be back in time for chores."

"Have fun." Steve smiled and went back to his book.

She heard Mary in the kitchen so she used the front door. It would be almost impossible to speak politely if Mary asked her about her afternoon plans.

Her hat shielded her eyes from the bright glare of the sun. Dust puffed onto her boots as she ran to the barn. She stopped at the sound of voices.

"Let's get out of here before Tina or Phil finds us together."

It was Dallas Tromley! Tina pressed against the side of the barn. Maybe she could learn something. Who was he talking to?

"Who cares if they know we're friends?"

Bridget Hawksley! Bridget and Dallas together! Tina locked her fingers together and waited breathlessly. When had the two of them met?

"They could keep me from coming to visit you. I wouldn't like that, would you?" Dallas's voice was soft and tender and it sickened Tina. He'd used that tone with her and she'd responded just the way he'd wanted.

Bridget laughed huskily. "I wouldn't want anything to keep you away. I just wish you could work with my daddy."

"I do too, but Steve Lambert wouldn't want a poor boy like me on his rich ranch."

Anger rose inside Tina and she had to force herself to stay quiet. A movement to her left brought her head around with a snap. Phil was sneaking around the tool shed, looking back over his shoulder. Tina frowned. Who was he trying to get away from? Did he know Dallas was in the barn right this minute with Bridget?

In a flash she was away from the barn and headed for the shed to tell Phil.

"Phil," she whispered urgently and he jumped in alarm. She saw a piece of white paper clutched in his hands. Her heart plummeted to her feet. It was the same paper that her notes had been written on. She pointed to the paper and he guiltily hid it behind his back.

"What's that?" she asked hoarsely.

"Nothing!"

"Show me, Phil!" She walked toward him and he backed away. "Show me right now!" Her mouth suddenly felt cotton dry and her heart beat loud enough for Phil to hear.

"You don't want to see it, Tina," he said sharply. "I don't want you to."

"Because I caught you in the act, Phil? You were hiding it so I'd find it tomorrow?" Oh, how could Phil be her enemy? A bitter taste filled her mouth and she thought she was going to be sick.

"What crazy talk is this? What do you mean, Tina?"

"You know very well what I mean!" What a good actor! To think she'd trusted him! Maybe she should run to the barn and ask Dallas for help.

Phil pushed his fingers through his blond curls. She knew he was very upset, probably about being caught with the evidence in his hand.

"I already know what's in the note, or about what's in it," she said with a scowl. "You might as well have the courage to hand it over to me face to face."

Slowly he held out his hand and she grabbed the paper. "I wish you wouldn't read it, Tina. It'll only scare you."

"Isn't that what you wanted?" She looked down at the bold words. *I know how I'm going to get even with you!*

"I was going to take it to Steve. I thought I saw someone sneaking around out here and I was trying to see who hid this in the shed."

She blinked. Was he trying to say he hadn't written the note, but had found it in the shed?

"Let's take it in right now and show it to Steve, Tina."

He started toward the house and she ran after him and caught his arm. "Wait, Phil."

"Why?"

"Did you write that note?" She watched the surprise, then anger on his face. She held her breath as she waited anxiously for his answer.

▪ SEVEN ▪

Oh, Phil!

Phil shook his head helplessly. "Oh, Tina. Tina. I wouldn't do that to you! I would never hurt you."

"You spanked me," she whispered.

"Only because I was so upset! I was scared of what would happen to you on a half-broken horse. Then when you finally got back, you jumped all over me. You didn't even give me a chance to find out if you were hurt."

She touched his arm. "I didn't get hurt."

"I know."

She looked down at the note clutched in her hand, then back up at him. "I'm sorry, Phil. I know you wouldn't write this to me. You wouldn't try to get even."

"I think Steve should know about the note." He turned toward the house but she caught his arm.

"Not yet, Phil. I think I know who's writing them."

"Them?" he asked sharply, his eyes narrowing. "You have others?"

She looked around nervously. "We can't talk here." Were Dallas and Bridget spying on them from inside the barn? She shoved the note into her pocket with the others. "Let's go sit on the porch."

Suddenly she realized Phil was looking past her with a scowl. She turned to follow his gaze and gasped as Dallas disappeared in the trees near the pond.

"What was he doing here?" Phil asked sharply.

"I heard him talking to Bridget a while ago. They're friends."

"I'm going to warn her about him. He's bad news wherever he goes." He started forward but Tina stopped him.

"We were going to talk." Was Bridget more important to him?

He hesitated. "I can talk to Bridget later."

The words brought a lift to her heart. She tugged on his hand and he walked across the driveway with her.

She kept the fear from her voice as she told him about the notes, then showed them to him. She watched his large suntanned hands as he spread out the notes and studied them. Finally he looked up.

"Why haven't you shown these to Steve?"

"I was going to, but he's always busy with Mary. I wanted to find out who was doing this to me first. If it's Bridget. . . ." Her voice faded away at the look on his face. "It could be her!"

He shook his head. "She isn't that kind of girl."

"Oh?" She told him that Bridget had tricked her into riding Charger just to get her into trouble. "If she'll do that, she'll do anything."

"I can't understand why you don't like her, Tina."

"I just don't! I can't help myself." She didn't like the sound of the words even as they left her mouth. Dad would tell her that she was to love everyone because God did. "Don't say anything, Phil. I couldn't stand a sermon right now."

He grinned. "I was thinking it, but I won't say anything."

She rubbed her hand down her jeans. "I thought maybe Dallas wrote them. He's mad enough at me. Today he threatened me. It could be him."

"I think so, too. He would do something mean like that."

Tina laughed. "You don't like Dallas any more than I like Bridget. Why is that, Phil?" Could she get him to admit that he was jealous?

"He's lazy. He'll do anything to get money, except work for it. He's stuck on himself. Want to hear more?" As he smiled, his teeth looked whiter against his sun-darkened face. "And you sneaked out to ride with him and let him kiss you. What're you laughing about? I know I'm just a little jealous. You don't have to rub it in, do you?"

"Phil, I'm sorry that I thought you wrote the notes. I knew you hadn't, but I was a little scared."

"I know." He fingered the torn pieces of paper. "I wonder if maybe Toad Myers did it. You know how big he is on practical jokes."

She nodded. "I wondered if one of the ranch hands could have, but it isn't very funny if it's supposed to be a joke."

"I'll see if Toad did it. He's the only one who might have."

"Do you think he'll admit to it?"

Phil rubbed his jaw thoughtfully. "I'll explain to him that you're scared about some notes you've been getting. If it's him, he'll say so. He wouldn't hurt anyone if he could help it."

Tina leaned against the step, her elbows resting on the porch floor, her face thoughtful. "I wanted to ask Bridget, but I know she'd lie."

Phil turned to her. "God knows who's doing this to you. Let's ask him to show us who it is and how to stop him."

Tina frowned. How would God let them know? Did Phil think God would talk to him or something?

"Tina, God is our heavenly Father. He cares

about what happens to you and to me. He can help us learn who's writing the notes. He wants to help us in our everyday life."

Tina looked at Phil in surprise. She knew that God had sent Jesus to save her, but did he really care about her problems every day? "I didn't know that. It makes me feel kind of . . . kind of strange." She locked her fingers together in her lap and stared down at her knees.

"Tina, you haven't been a Christian very long. You need to get better acquainted with your heavenly Father. Find out about him by reading your Bible. I'll show you verses that tell that he cares more for you than the flowers and birds and other things he made."

She listened in awe as he talked, interrupting now and then to ask him a question. No wonder Dad said being a Christian was the most important thing that ever happened to him. No wonder Mary talked to God all the time as if he walked right beside her.

By the time they finished talking and Phil had prayed, Tina knew they would learn who was writing the notes, that he'd stop harassing her.

Who would have thought that God could love her; a rich rancher's spoiled little daughter with a bad temper and a mean streak as wide as the barn?

With tears sparkling in her eyes she pushed the notes into her jeans and stood up. "I can't wait to find out who my enemy is, Phil. I'm going to get him or her good!"

Phil shook his head as he stood beside her, his thumbs looped in his front pockets. "Tina. Tina. Jesus said to love your enemies and do good to those who do harm to you."

"What?" she shrieked. "That's too much to expect!"

"You'll learn. Jesus also said to forgive."

"Are you sure?" She frowned up at him. She could not forgive the one scaring her.

"I'll show you in your Bible if you want."

"Not today, Phil. I'm sure not ready for that today."

He started to speak but before he could the door behind them opened and Steve and Mary walked out.

"Howdy, kids," said Steve with a smile. "We were just coming to find you. We would like the two of you to put on a show for us. Mary hasn't seen what you can do on Blaze and Ginger."

"Only if you want to," said Mary. "And if you won't get hurt."

Tina tossed her head. "We can't get hurt. We're too good at trick riding, aren't we, Phil?"

"I knew you'd agree," cut in Steve before Phil could answer. "I called Slim and asked him to have Blaze and Ginger saddled and ready and to tell the boys that there's going to be a show."

Tina wrinkled her nose at Steve. "What if I'd said no?"

"Oh, Tina, you can't any more turn down an offer to show off than you can quit breathing." Steve tugged her ponytail and she laughed.

"Let's get the show on the road, Tina," said Phil as he leaped down the porch steps to land beside the rosebushes. "Race you to the barn."

She sped along after him, but his long legs were no match for her short ones. Bridget just had to be watching, watching with envy!

Tina hugged Blaze and pressed her face against his neck. What would she do without Blaze? He belonged to her. Dad had given him to her after Mother died. It was his way of trying to take her mind off her heartache.

She scratched down the white blaze on his face, then rubbed around his black ears. "Ready to show off, Blaze?" She looked around at the ranch hands standing beside the fence. Good! Bridget stood with Hawk near Toad Myers.

Tina waited for Phil's signal, then leaped into the saddle. With precise movements one trick followed another. She heard the shouts and whistles as she stood on her shoulder, her feet high in the air, her toes pointed gracefully. She knew Phil was to her left doing the same trick on Ginger. Finally they dismounted with a flourish, their hands high in the air.

Suddenly Mary grabbed Tina's arms in a tight grip. "You are never doing that again! Do you hear me?"

Tina blinked in surprise. "What are you talking about?"

"You scared me to death, Tina Lambert. You could've been killed."

"Now, Mary," said Steve pulling her tightly into his arms. "Tina has been trick riding since she was five years old. She's not going to get hurt."

Tina's mouth dropped open. Why was Mary scared?

Mary shivered as she pushed away from Steve. "I guess there are some things I'll have to get used to, living in this family. My heart is still in my mouth."

"Mary, I won't get hurt," said Tina hesitantly, awkwardly. "It's no different to me than walking. Honest."

"Oh, Phil! You were wonderful!" cried Bridget.

Tina's face flamed and she had to force herself to stand still. Why didn't Bridget keep her hands off Phil? Did she always have to hug him that way? Did he like it?

Hawk caught Tina's hand tightly and shook it. "You were some rider, little Tina. I reckon I can trust you on any horse I train."

Tina swelled with pride. Coming from

Hawk, it was high praise. "I wouldn't ride half-broken horses, Hawk."

"I think you could," he answered with a grin, his hat in his hands. "I think you could ride anything if you had to."

"But she won't," said Steve, tugging the ponytail over Tina's left ear. "She'll stick with Blaze. Right, honey?"

"Right, Dad."

Hawk's praise left a warm glow around her heart even when Bridget led Phil toward the corral.

Toad Myers caught up Blaze's reins while another man held Ginger's. "You're a mighty brave girl, Tina," said Toad with a grin. "Mighty brave."

"Thank you," she said with a slight smile. She studied the young cowboy as he started past her leading Blaze. Had Toad written the notes?

"Watch out by your foot, Tina!" Toad stopped and pointed, his eyes popped out more than usual.

Tina leaped back at the sight of the snake at her feet. She stifled a scream, her eyes wide in fear.

"Not so brave after all, huh, Tina?" asked Toad as he bent down and picked up the snake. "A little 'ole rubber snake can't hurt you." He roared with laughter, slapping his thigh with glee. "I caught you good that time, Tina Lambert. I reckon I did."

"It wasn't funny, Toad," Tina said over the laughter of the others. "You know snakes scare me."

"I couldn't let you get too big for yer britches, could I?" He chuckled as he walked away with Blaze.

"Don't let him upset you, honey," said Steve as he slid a long arm around her slender shoulders. "You know Toad. He doesn't mean any harm."

"I'm not so sure," she said to herself thoughtfully as she remembered just a couple of weeks ago how angry he'd been with her because she wouldn't go to town to the show with him.

Maybe Toad's jokes weren't just to be funny. Maybe he used that way to get back at anyone who upset him.

Tina touched her pocket and the notes crackled. Maybe Toad had written the notes. If he had, then she had nothing to worry about. He wouldn't go any further than to write the notes to scare her. He wouldn't do anything to physically harm her. Would he?

EIGHT

A Talk
with Mary

"Steve, I don't know why you allow that cowboy to scare Tina that way," said Mary as they stepped into the house.

Tina stared at Mary in surprise.

"Don't let it bother you, Mary," said Steve, kissing the top of her head. "Tina's tough."

"So you keep telling me," said Mary dryly.

Tina filled a glass with cold water. Steve said he'd be in his study if they wanted him for anything.

The cold water slipped down her parched throat and washed away the dry dust.

"Can we talk for a few minutes, Tina?" asked Mary, a very serious look on her face.

Tina sank to a kitchen chair and waited. Mary was certainly acting strange. "What did I do wrong this time?" asked Tina sharply.

Mary sat down across from Tina and picked up a petal that had fallen from the vase of red roses. "Tina, you're a young woman. You're not a rough, tough cowboy. I think it's time you started walking and talking and acting like a girl instead of a boy."

"What?" she cried in surprise. Nobody would think she was a boy! She hadn't been boy-thin in a long time, almost a year now. Girls she knew envied her! What was Mary talking about?

"Tina, I didn't like the way Toad Myers scared you with that snake. It was out of place. You're too old for the ranch hands to treat you like one of the boys."

Tina rubbed her flushed cheeks. "They know I'm Steve Lambert's daughter."

Mary sighed and shook her head. "I know I'm not doing this very well. I just want you to be aware of a few things. Your dad has done a fine job raising you, but you need a woman's touch now. You need to put aside some of your freedoms with the ranch hands and hold yourself apart." Mary pushed back her dark curls.

"Tina, I guess what I'm trying to do is warn you. Steve and Slim don't know the men they hire. They don't know that they can be trusted around a young girl developing into woman-hood." She reached for Tina's hand.

"I just don't like the way that man, Toad Myers, looked at you today. It wouldn't be wise to be alone with him."

Tina cleared her throat. Mary was scaring

her. She'd never thought about Toad or the others hurting her or thinking of her as a woman even though she looked older than thirteen. "Dad wouldn't let them touch me, Mary."

"He couldn't stop them if he wasn't here. And Phil isn't always around to help you either." She squeezed Tina's hand, then released it. "I don't want to scare you. I just want you to be aware of the possible danger to you."

Tina thought of the notes and pressed her hand against her pocket. Was she in real danger? Oh, why wasn't life simple the way it once was?

"Another thing, Tina," said Mary hesitantly. "I'm sorry for getting upset about your trick riding. My heart was in my mouth the whole time. I know it's my problem and I won't bother you with it again."

Tina's eyes widened. She had never had a mother's concern since Mother had died. Did Mary really feel like a mother toward her? Did she really love her the way she said she did?

"Tina, now that I have a family, I don't want anything to happen to it. You and Steve are my life now."

Tina rubbed her hand across the oak table top. "Mary, I said I would learn to love you as my mother. I . . . I don't think I've been trying very hard lately." She looked up and caught the glad look on Mary's face. "I want to be a family. I really do, but something always stops me from it. I want to be a good Christian, but something keeps me from being one. I do bad things and I just can't help myself."

"Tina, do you know that you have an enemy?"

Tina locked her fingers in her lap and leaned forward. Did Mary know about the notes?

"Don't look so surprised and scared, honey. You know that God loves you, that Jesus is your Savior. Since you sided with God, Satan is your enemy."

"Oh, that!" She knew about Satan. She'd heard people talk about him and say he made them do wrong.

"Don't shrug it away so lightly, Tina." Mary rubbed her hands up and down her arms. "Jesus wants us to learn to fight against Satan. We are in a spiritual battle here on earth. We must take God's armor and his weapons and fight the battle.

"Tina, any time a Christian learns something new about God, Satan tries to steal it out of our hearts. We must be aware of this and stand against it by quoting God's Word during any test or trial that comes our way."

Mary pushed back her chair and jumped up. "I just realized something! I have been learning that God is always with us and will always protect us if we trust him to. Satan came along with fear for you to take the trust for God out of my heart.

"Fear is not from God, Tina! If you're ever afraid, it is Satan's doing and you don't have to accept it. Fear is the opposite of faith." She pressed her hands together in front of her. "I reject this fear I felt for you, Tina. I know God is protecting you. I know he has given his angels charge over you and that no harm will come to you."

Tears stung Tina's eyes as she realized what Mary was telling her. "You mean I never have to be afraid?" She wanted to show Mary the notes but she couldn't bring herself to do it.

"The Bible says that perfect love casts out fear. That means if we have a total love toward God and know that he loves us in return, we have nothing to fear, because he is right with us to take care of us." Mary dropped back on her chair and sat with her elbows on the table, her chin in her hands. "Tina, it's so exciting to me when God shows me part of himself. And I refuse to let Satan steal God's Word from me!"

Tina shifted on her chair. "Mary, show me in the Bible where it tells about God's fighting gear for us."

Mary chuckled as she lifted her Bible off the counter beside the radio. "It's the sixth chapter of Ephesians that talks about the armor of God. Here it is." She sat in a chair beside Tina and moved her Bible so they could both read.

As Mary explained about the armor, Tina

listened with deep interest. She would fight Satan and the person writing the notes. But she wouldn't do it with angry words or fists. She would do her best to use God's words to fight with.

Mary showed her in the Gospels how Jesus had fought against Satan in the wilderness. She showed Tina that each time Satan tempted Jesus, Jesus answered with Scripture.

"Tina, that's why it's important to learn God's Word. Satan must flee when you quote God's words to him.

"You said that you wanted to be good, but couldn't. Tina, in yourself you can only be bad, but since you have God's nature inside you, you can be good.

"If you're tempted to be bad, just stand against it and say that you are a new creature in Christ, that your old nature is dead, and you have a new nature."

Tina listened closely, not wanting to miss a single word from Mary. Phil had said that God wanted to help her live each day. He wasn't just a God sitting up in heaven a trillion miles away. He was her heavenly Father who loved her and wanted her love in return. Just as Steve helped her each day in ordinary daily things, her heavenly Father wanted to help her even more.

Jesus was her brother, her friend. The Holy Spirit was her comforter, her teacher. She had a heavenly family who loved her!

For the first time since the day she'd accepted Jesus as her Savior a peace filled her heart. Love surged through her and she hugged Mary.

"I'm glad you're my mother, Mary. Thank you for talking to me. I will read my Bible and talk to my heavenly Father from now on. I guess I didn't know it was so important."

"We'll talk again, Tina," said Mary, rubbing tears off her cheeks. "I enjoy sharing God's Word with you."

"You make it easy to understand."

"No, honey. The Holy Spirit makes it easy to understand. That's part of his job."

Tina held Mary's Bible close to her, her eyes sparkling. She knew that in this Book were the answers she'd need to be the person she wanted to be. As soon as she got back to her room, she'd talk to her heavenly Father about the threatening notes she'd received. And maybe she'd see what the Bible said about forgiveness.

NINE

Blaze
Disappears

Tina hummed happily as she walked toward the barn to take Blaze from his stall to put him in the corral. The ranch was buzzing with activity while the men prepared to leave on their various jobs, and Tina waved to them. Two days had gone by without a threatening note and she felt very free and unafraid.

Just as she opened the barn door Toad Myers jumped out, startling her.

"Don't do that, Toad," she said sharply.

He slapped his thigh and laughed. "You're sure jumpy, Tina. Why is that?"

She shrugged, wondering if Phil had talked to Toad yet about the notes. She lifted her chin and stepped forward. "Please excuse me, Toad. I have to take care of Blaze."

He caught her arm and fear leaped inside her. "You can't walk past me as if I wasn't here. You give Phil plenty of time. Why not me? I'm older and wiser than Phil. You'd know you'd been kissed if I kissed you."

"Let me go," she said harshly. What had Mary said to do when she was afraid? Oh, she couldn't remember!

"Am I hurting you?" he asked softly, his grip loosening a fraction. "I sure don't want to hurt you. I just want a kiss."

Tina's foot flew forward and her boot connected with Toad's shin. He cried in pain, dropping her wrist and leaping around holding his leg.

"You touch me again and I'll talk to Dad. Understand?"

"You'll be sorry," he muttered with an angry scowl. "You will sure be sorry!" He almost ran toward the bunkhouse, his short legs pumping up and down, his arms swinging hard backward and forward.

Tina leaned weakly against the side of the barn. She had never had trouble with the ranch hands. Why couldn't Toad leave her alone? If he didn't she would have to tell Dad.

She looked toward the house. Maybe she should tell Mary, or maybe follow Dad to the north pasture and tell him.

Nervously she rubbed her hands down her jeans. What had Mary showed her in the Bible about God's protection?

Tina frowned. She couldn't remember what the verses had said, but she knew that God said he was always with her, watching over her. She would not allow herself to be afraid of Toad.

"Thank you, heavenly Father, for your protection. Keep Toad away from me." A barn cat rubbed against her leg and she bent to pick him up. He was soft and furry against her cheek. She heard his purring and felt the vibration against her hands.

All at once she knew that just as the cat was safe in her hands, she was safe in God's hands. She belonged to him. He always took care of her. She smiled as she set the cat on the hard-packed dirt floor.

Just then someone called to her from outdoors. She poked her head out the door into the bright morning sunlight and squinted to see who had shouted. It was Toad and she frowned.

"Tina, I forgot to tell you that Phil said to meet him in the pines as soon as possible."

She lifted her hand to acknowledge that she'd heard. She'd saddle Blaze, tell Mary where she was going, then ride to meet Phil. Maybe he'd learned something important and wanted to tell her immediately.

She stopped outside Blaze's stall and stared in surprise. He wasn't there. "Don't panic," she whispered to herself. "Maybe someone let him out already."

She dashed outdoors and stood at the corral gate and watched the horses milling around. Blaze was not there. Would Phil have taken Blaze? She shook her head hard. No! Never! Phil knew Blaze was her horse.

Maybe Blaze had been stolen!

She groaned and sagged weakly against the fence. But why Blaze and not all the other horses? "To get even with me!" she whispered hoarsely.

The cat mewed inside the barn and she remembered about being in God's hands. She looked up, tears stinging her eyes. "Heavenly Father, help me to find Blaze. Don't let any harm come to him. Take real good care of him, please." She knuckled away her tears. "Thank you, Father, in Jesus' name."

Just then Hawk walked past leading Charger. Tina dashed to his side and walked along beside him as she eagerly asked him if he'd seen Blaze.

Hawk shook his head, his face in shadow from his hat. "Can't help you none, little friend. But I wouldn't worry at all if I was you. He'll turn up."

"How can you be so sure?" The words brought a wild hope leaping inside her.

"Who would take just Blaze and not another horse? Take Charger here." He nodded in the direction of the big black gelding. "Charger is worth a lot of money. If somebody wanted to steal something valuable, they would've taken him."

She gnawed the inside of her lower lip. "But . . . but what if someone wanted to hurt me?"

"Who'd want that?" He pushed his hat to the back of his head and looked down at her. "Has my girl been up to no good again?"

Her eyes widened. "You mean you believed me when I said she told me to take Charger?"

"I reckon I didn't want to believe she did that. I was talkin' about somethin' else."

"Oh!" She moistened her dry lips with the tip of her tongue. "What were you talking about?"

"I sure shouldn't tell you, but I will." He stopped, his hold firm on Charger's bridle as he looked down at her. "She bet Toad Myers that he couldn't make you kiss him."

"She what?" Her voice came out in a high squeak.

"She bet him that he couldn't sweet-talk you or scare you into kissing him. He said he could. I told him to keep away from you, so maybe you don't need to worry about it."

"He tried all right. I kicked him in the shin."

Hawk threw back his head and laughed loud and long and finally Tina joined in.

"Your daddy don't have to worry about you," he said with a wink. "You can sure take care of yourself."

The smile left her face. "Where do you think Blaze is?"

He shook his head, took his hat off and scratched his dark head. "I don't know, Tina. If he don't turn up before late afternoon, I'll help you look for him. He could've run off."

"Not Blaze! He's trained to stay unless I give him a command to leave."

"Could be Phil has him. I haven't seen him this morning."

"Phil would never take Blaze without checking with me first."

"Don't get yourself riled. Blaze will turn up. Just wait and see." He settled his hat in place and walked on with Charger.

Tina stood, uncertain what to do next. Maybe Hawk was right. Maybe Phil had taken Blaze and wanted her to meet him in the pines to explain why.

Should she take the time to tell Mary where she was going? She frowned. It was hard to consider Mary's feelings and wishes. Dad had mostly left her on her own.

"I guess I'd better tell her," she said with a sigh. Dad would be mad if Mary worried about her.

"Can't this wait, Tina?" Mary asked, looking up from the piano she was dusting. "I thought we might go to town to buy school clothes for you."

"School clothes? I can get those any time."

"I want us to go together and make a day of it." Mary smiled. "Maybe we could take Bridget with us. She doesn't have a mother to help her buy clothes."

Tina twisted her toe in the carpet. She had never had anyone but the saleslady help her buy clothes before. It might be fun going with Mary, but certainly not with Bridget!

"Mary, don't be mad or anything, but I've got to meet Phil in the pines right now. Maybe we can shop tomorrow."

"Tomorrow I have to spend the day in school for an in-service meeting. I heard that I'll have twenty-seven children in my kindergarten room this year. That's a lot of little people for one room. But maybe we could go the day after."

"All right." Tina hesitated. "Could we go without Bridget?"

"Of course. It would be fun, just the two of us."

Tina walked to the door, then looked over her shoulder to smile and say she'd see Mary later.

"Steve won't be back for lunch, Tina, so don't you desert me too. I hate to eat alone." She grinned. "I guess I had too much of that before I married your dad."

"See you at lunch."

In just a few minutes Tina had Ginger saddled and sat astride the big mare. Tina frowned. No horse was missing aside from Colonel and Dad had him. Phil must have taken Blaze. But why?

An uneasiness settled over Tina as she rode from the yard toward the pines. Before long she'd know what Phil wanted and why he'd taken Blaze, if he had.

A gentle breeze blew against her and she remembered the first time she'd sneaked out to meet Dallas Tromley. How stupid she'd been! But at the time she'd been excited and happy.

Suddenly Tina stiffened in the saddle, then looked quickly around. What if her enemy was watching her right now just waiting for this time to get her alone. She shook her head, making the ponytails over her ears flop. Phil would never ask her to meet him in the pines if he thought there was danger.

TEN

A Meeting in the Pines

A dog barked nearby and Tina lifted her head to listen. It had to be Jim Bridger, and where Jim Bridger was, Codge Farenholz must be close by.

Tina turned Ginger toward the line fence between their ranch and Codge's ranch. It had been a while since she'd seen her friend.

Just as Tina reached the barbed wire fence Codge walked up with his dog beside him. Jim Bridger barked a short, sharp welcome and Tina said hello to him.

"You're looking prettier than a field of sunflowers, Tina," said Codge with a chuckle. "What brings you riding out here this early in the morning?" He stood with his jean-clad legs apart, his hands lightly on his hips. His floppy hat was pushed to the back of his balding head.

She told him about meeting Phil in the

pines, and about her scare when Blaze was not in his stall.

Codge took off his hat and rubbed his head, a frown wrinkling his forehead. His face looked like old leather. "Something's mighty funny, little girl. I could swear I saw Phil in the pickup this morning with Smokey, heading for town. You sure you didn't get yer wires crossed somewhere?"

"I hope not!" She shook her head. "No. I'm sure Phil didn't go to town. I'm sure he's waiting at the pines for me."

Codge settled his floppy hat in place and dropped his hand on Jim Bridger's head. "I hate to think my sight is failing me. But me and Jim Bridger ain't gettin' no younger."

"Don't tell me that, you faker. You know you're as young and spry as any of the cowboys on our place." She looked down at Codge with a smile. "You take care of yourself and Jim Bridger."

"Tell Steve I'll be over directly to show him a silver-studded bridle I got last auction. He might be interested in buying it."

"I'll tell him. He's gone for the day, but he'll be back for supper."

Codge nodded and she lifted her hand, then turned Ginger and rode away. Jim Bridger barked again, then all was quiet except for the muted hoofbeats of Ginger and a few birds.

Tina squinted as she looked toward the pines. Was Phil there? Or had Toad given her a wrong message? She shook her head. He had no reason to do that. Her eyes widened and she slowed Ginger. Maybe Toad meant to follow her out to get her alone!

"Tina. Tina, you're only asking for trouble," she said to herself. "You're gonna start thinking there's a rattler under every rock."

Ginger nickered and bobbed her head.

Someone was definitely in the pines with a horse. Was it Phil with Blaze? Whoever was there had seen her right out in full view in the middle of the open prairie. Maybe it would've been better if she'd swung around the other way and came up from behind.

She bumped Ginger with her knees and started forward. She'd see who was at the pines and if it wasn't Phil, she'd ride away fast.

A shiver ran up and down her spine as she stopped at the edge of the pines. She cupped her hands around her mouth. "Phil! Phil, I'm here!" She waited, her ears tuned to hear every movement.

A twig snapped and she jumped.

"I'm here, Tina!"

The call was muffled.

"Come meet me," she called back.

"Come here, Tina. I want to show you something."

She frowned. Was it Phil's voice? She

couldn't tell. She moved to dismount, then stopped. "Show yourself first, Phil! I won't dismount until I see you."

She waited, her eyes glued to the spot where she'd heard his voice. Why wasn't he walking toward her in plain sight? Was he playing some game with her?

"I'm here, Tina."

Her head snapped around and her eyes flew wide open. "Dallas!" He sat astride Molly just a way behind her. "Where's Phil?"

He shrugged. "I sure don't know. I came out here to meet you. We have some unfinished business to take care of." He rode forward, a satisfied smile on his face.

Tina shouted to Ginger and leaned forward as Ginger broke into a run. Blaze could outrun Molly, but could Ginger?

"You won't get away, Tina!" shouted Dallas as he pulled up beside her and reached down for Ginger's bridle.

Tina kicked out of the stirrups and flung herself off Ginger, hitting the ground on her feet. She ran toward the pines, desperately trying to reach shelter before Dallas could catch her. In the pines she could hide.

Sounds of pounding hooves close behind her sent her heart racing wildly. Urgently she called out for her heavenly Father to protect her from harm.

"Give up, Tina. I've got you."

She felt Molly's breath on her back and she

wondered if Dallas meant to run her down. She jumped aside and looked up just as Dallas leaped from the saddle straight at her. She stumbled and he fell on her, knocking her to the ground with a sickening thud.

"You lose, Tina Lambert. The rich rancher's daughter has fallen!" Dallas chucked as he rolled off her, catching her arm tightly as she struggled to stand up.

"Let me go! Do you hear me?" She kicked and fought but he kept her at arm's length and she couldn't touch him.

"I've been planning this for a long time, my girl." He pulled her to her feet and held her arms tightly as he looked down into her face. Her hair hung in tangles around her scratched face. Her shirt tail hung out of her jeans.

She stared defiantly up at him. "Planning what?" She had to know the worst.

"You'll know soon enough. Let's go sit down in the shade of the pines and talk a while. I sure don't want anybody seeing us together." He looked back over his shoulder with a frown. "I heard that dog of Codge Farenholz bark a while ago. He'd better not be spying on us if he knows what's good for him."

Tina wished with all her might that Codge and Jim Bridger would decide to walk over to the pines. But what could the short, wiry man do to Dallas? But with both Jim Bridger and Codge, Dallas wouldn't stand a chance.

A tall pine shut out the hot rays of the sun

and Dallas pushed Tina to the ground to sit on the pine needles under the tree.

"Now, we'll talk." He sat crosslegged in front of her, his hands resting lightly on his legs.

She sat with her back pressed against the tree, her knees under her chin. How could she get away?

"I'm surprised you came today, Tina. I was afraid my plan wouldn't work." Dallas grinned and she wanted to slap his face.

"I thought I was meeting Phil." She wrapped her arms around her legs and forced the shivers away.

"Bridget said she'd give you a message for me."

"Bridget? But Toad Myers told me to come out here."

Dallas slapped his leg. "Leave it to Bridget to think of a sure way. She said you wouldn't believe her if she told you."

Tina's eyes flashed. "I wouldn't have, either!"

"She told me what she's been up to. I think she hates you almost as much as I do."

"I suppose *you* wrote the notes to scare me."

He nodded. "I thought you might think it was me. I was going to write more of them just to keep you really scared, then I decided that wasn't enough."

She gnawed her lower lip in agitation.

"Don't get so scared. I'm not going to hurt

you. I'm not crazy enough to do that and have Steve Lambert on my back forever." He tapped her booted toes. "I'm not even going to kiss you. I can get all the kisses I want from Bridget."

"What do you want?" she asked hoarsely. Why couldn't she act calm and unafraid? He was taking this long to tell her what he had in mind just to torment her. She hated for him to know that she was scared.

"I'll get to that in a minute." He pushed his fingers through his dark brown hair. His brown eyes glowed with excitement. "This is a sure way of making money."

"You aren't going to rob Codge, are you?" she asked in alarm.

"No. I heard the crazy old coot put all his money in the bank after we tried to rob him."

She sagged in relief. "I'm glad! I wish he would've pressed charges against you and Carl and Larry. Then you'd be in jail now where you couldn't hurt anyone."

His face darkened with anger. "And where would that leave Ma? Don't you care that she'd be on her own in that run-down house on that no-good ranch she bought?"

Tina leaned forward. "You don't care, Dallas! You could help her work the place and make it into something, but you're busy running around trying to find a way to make quick, easy money."

"I'm doing it for Ma!" He locked his fingers

together and cracked his knuckles loudly. "All we need is a little money and we can get out of here. She shouldn't have to work so hard."

"She wanted to buy that place, Dallas. She wants to live there. You're the one who's so crazy to get back to the city."

"Not everybody's cut out to live in the country and like it. Not everybody is like you, Tina. And not all ranchers make the kind of money Steve Lambert makes by selling his trained horses."

"He works hard, Dallas! You know he does. He doesn't expect anything for free like you do."

Dallas leaped to his feet, his fists doubled at his sides. "Shut up! I'm working for what I get!"

Tina kicked out with all her strength and caught him by surprise as her boots smashed into his legs. He fell hard and she leaped up and raced away, wildly looking for Ginger. Oh, if only Blaze were here! Blaze would run to her at a whistle and she'd mount while he was running and be gone before Dallas stood to his feet.

Ginger stood out in the open, her nose buried in the grass. Molly stood grazing beside her.

"You can't get away, Tina!" cried Dallas angrily. "You're dumb to try. When I catch you, it'll go harder for you."

The words rang inside her head as she ran around another tree. Oh, where could she hide?

Sounds of breaking twigs and footsteps sent a burst of speed to her legs.

Could she climb a tree quickly and make him think she'd run on? But the branches started high over her head and she could not reach one even if she jumped.

She flung herself around a bush and hid. In agony she watched Dallas race past. Her breast rose and fell and her lungs ached. The minute he was out of sight she ran back the way she came. She had to reach Ginger and get home where she'd be safe!

A sharp pain shot through her side but she forced herself to keep running. Just as she reached the edge of the pines she heard Dallas shout to her.

Her heart dropped to her feet and fear pricked her skin. Dallas was close behind her again!

She felt his arms close around her legs and she fell to the ground. With a sob she lay still, waiting for him to make the next move.

▪ ELEVEN ▪

Dallas's Diabolical Plan

Tina choked back a sob as Dallas pushed her down hard. She struck her head a glancing blow against the trunk of a tall pine.

"You'll get worse than that if you run away from me again." Dallas dropped to the ground in front of her, his face set. "You don't know how close you came to getting hurt. If I didn't have plans for you, you'd have a broken neck right now."

She shivered. Did he mean it or was he stretching the truth just to scare her? "Why don't you just tell me your plan and get it over with?"

"Give me time," he said with a frown as he looked at his watch.

She locked her fingers together around her knees. Was he stalling for time for a reason?

Suddenly Dallas chuckled and Tina stared at him in surprise. What made him laugh? She saw him brush an ant off his leg.

"I wish I could've seen your face when you found that first note I wrote you, Tina. I figured you'd think it was a joke, then you'd start worrying about it.

Tina squirmed in agitation. How she wanted to leap at him and stop his grin!

"I think the note I put in your Bible was the most challenging." He nodded. "Yes, that was the one. I picked up your Bible and slipped in the note. Mary almost caught me with it, but I quickly dropped it on her Bible next to her purse. She picked up both Bibles without thinking anything about it."

"I should've known it was you!" She glared at him, her blue eyes dark. "I thought it might be, but I wasn't sure."

"I tried to get you to say something about the notes when I scared you in the Sunday school room. But you didn't say a word."

"Because I thought Bridget was doing it!"

"That's funny! Bridget! She's not smart enough to do that." He leaned forward. "You almost caught me putting the note under your saddle. I saw how scared you were. I laughed so hard I thought for sure you'd hear me."

Her cheeks flushed red and she wanted to sink out of sight. To think he had been watching her! And how many times had he heard her telling her secret thoughts and feelings to Blaze?

"It's time."

She gasped, her hand at her throat. "Time for what?"

He grinned. "Did I say time? I meant I am going to tell you my plan. Before tonight I'll have the money I need for Ma and me."

She pounded her fists on the ground. "I told you that I can't get money."

"Who said anything about you getting money for me?" He picked up a handful of pine needles and poured them from one hand to the other, then dropped them. "You are going to ride Charger to my house and put him in my barn."

"What?" Her voice seemed loud in the stillness. "I won't!"

"Tina, you will!" His eyes narrowed. "I have a buyer coming for him."

She tried to jump up but he caught her and pushed her back down. Her heart raced and her brain whirled with ways to escape.

"You're going to ride Ginger home right now, saddle Charger, and ride him to my place. If you aren't there by just past noon, I'll kill Blaze."

"Blaze!" She swallowed hard. "*You* have Blaze!"

He nodded. "I had to have a sure way to make you bring me Charger. He'll sell for a lot of money. Bridget said so."

"Did she know about this?"

He shook his head. "I wouldn't tell her my plans. She'd blab them all over to whoever would listen." He shook his head again. "No. I sure wouldn't tell Bridget."

"How . . . how did you get Blaze without anyone seeing you?" Tina felt scalding tears rise inside her and she forced them back. She would not break down and cry in front of Dallas!

"It was easy. He didn't give me a bit of trouble."

"I can't believe that! Did you have to use a whip on him to make him obey you? He's trained to obey only me."

"Don't you worry, Tina. He's in my barn as healthy as when you saw him yesterday." He jumped up and pulled her up beside him. Her legs felt like rubber and she almost fell.

"I won't take Charger for you, Dallas," she said in a low, tense voice. She smelled the pine trees and Dallas's perspiration. "You can't make me exchange Blaze for Charger."

"Can't I?" he asked in a deadly calm voice. "Are you sure?"

"When I get home, I'll tell Dad that you have Blaze and he'll get him away from you."

"Tina, your dad won't be home until supper time. I found that out from Bridget. She didn't know how much help she was being when she told me the actions of everyone today." He laughed dryly. "She thought I was interested in her life."

Tina stamped her foot in frustration. How could she save both Blaze and Charger? There had to be a way!

"Before you get any more wild ideas, Tina

Lambert, I have one more surprise for you. I have Phil tied up right now in my barn with Blaze. He will stay there until you bring me Charger. If you don't bring Charger to me on time, Phil will die right along with Blaze."

"Oh, Dallas! Would you really do that?"

"Easy. I hate Phil." He forced her to walk with him toward the mares. "You climb right up on Ginger and ride for home. Leave Ginger and ride Charger to my place. I know how much time it'll take you. If you are even ten minutes late, Blaze and Phil will be dead and it'll be your fault." His grip tightened on her arm and she cried out. "And if you call the police, I'll kill them before the police can get to them and me. I'm desperate, Tina. I'll do anything for that money."

"Oh, I wish Codge had pressed charges against you and had you jailed! How can you live with yourself? How can you face your mother after all of this?"

"Very dramatic. You must've watched too much TV."

"Please, don't do this, Dallas! Please! Think about what you've been learning in church. God loves you!"

"Sure. Sure. He loved me so much he left me without a pa all these years."

"God didn't make him leave. God isn't keeping him away. God is good."

"What a little preacher! Just a few weeks ago you were as down on God as I am. My, my what a little religion will do to change a wild cat."

Ginger nickered, her head up as Tina was pushed toward her. Tina tried to hold back. There had to be a way out of this!

"Get on Ginger right now, Tina. I mean it! I'll be watching your every move. If you want to keep your precious horse and your hero alive, you'll follow my instructions."

Woodenly she mounted. She brushed back her tangled hair. The hot sun blazed down on her and she wished she'd worn her hat. She looked down at Dallas. "Please, don't do this! It's not too late."

"Get going! I can't stand your whining. I didn't think the day would come that Tina Lambert would beg."

She squared her shoulders and looked toward home. She would find a way to stop Dallas. She didn't know how right now, but she'd find a way!

"I know you think you can stop me, but you can't. I have it all under control, thanks to Bridget. You'll see." He stepped away from Ginger. "See you later, Tina. Have fun riding Charger." He chuckled.

"You'll be sorry for this, Dallas." It was hard to get the words out around the lump in her throat.

A gentle wind blew her hair back as she rode toward the ranch.

"You'd better go faster than that, Tina,"

shouted Dallas. "You have a deadline, you know."

Tina urged Ginger into a run. Somehow she had to stop Dallas. There had to be a way!

TWELVE

Charger

Tina turned Ginger into the almost empty corral beside the barn, then looked frantically around for help. Slim would be here, or Hawk, or one of the hands. Even Toad Myers would be of help right now.

With a frown Tina dashed toward the bunkhouse. Where were the men? Why was it so quiet around the place?

"Is anyone here?" she shouted as she ran. "Help me!" Oh, of all days for everyone to be gone! Maybe she should run in and get Mary. But what could she do?

Tears stung her eyes but she refused to let them fall as she ran to the corral where Charger was kept. He stood at the tank, his nose in the water. He lifted his great black head as Tina called to him.

Tina leaned against the gate and forced herself to calm down. She could not dash into the corral and scare Charger or she'd never catch him. She dare not let him sense her nervousness. All she had to do was walk up to him and catch him by the halter strap. Would he toss his head and knock her off her feet? Charger was used to Hawk and Phil, not her.

"Help, me, Father," she whispered urgently as she slowly walked across the dusty corral.

Charger dance-stepped around, then stopped, eyeing her.

"I won't hurt you, Charger. I need you right now. Please don't give me any trouble. Keep calm. I have to save Phil and Blaze. I sure don't want to do this, but I must." The lead rope felt heavy in her hand as she walked closer and closer. He jumped away from her and she wanted to scream in frustration. How much time had she wasted already by trying to find someone to help her?

"Whoa, Charger! Stand still!"

The big black gelding nodded his head up and down, then stood quietly. She knew he wanted to bolt, but he stood his ground and she was thankful that Hawk had trained him so well.

Thankfully she clicked the lead rope in place and led him to the gate. He was taller than Blaze, and harder to saddle because of it.

Tina looked frantically around again. Why hadn't anyone come to investigate? Everyone knew she wasn't to touch Charger. Someone should stop her!

But no one came and no one stopped her.

She rode across the yard to the open pasture. She kept a tight rein. This time she couldn't afford to let Charger take the bit. She had to have him under complete control.

A cottontail hopped away and startled Charger. Tina fought for a firm hold and managed to keep it.

Why hadn't Mary at least poked her head out the door to check on her? Why had the place been deserted? Was that part of Dallas's doing?

She could tell by the sun that it was almost noon. She didn't have much time. Her stomach tightened in a hard knot and she moaned.

Bending low, Tina urged Charger into a run. She knew his powerful legs would make short work of the distance between their place and Tromley's.

As she rode through Codge's property she willed him to see her, hear her, and follow her. But if Dallas saw that old red flatbed truck drive in, he'd know it was help for her, and she'd be in terrible trouble. Jim Bridger must not hear her and bark a warning to Codge. It would be too dangerous for Phil and Blaze for her to bring help.

A bitter taste filled her mouth and a shiver ran up and down her spine. How could she save Charger as well as Phil and Blaze?

She slowed Charger to a walk as she reached the Tromley lane. One lone tree shaded the weathered-gray house. Nothing moved except the leaves on the cottonwood tree.

She licked her dry lips as she rode toward the dilapidated gray barn. Was Dallas waiting inside to see that no one was following her before he dared to show himself?

"Whoa, Charger," she said in a low, hoarse voice. She wanted to turn Charger and ride fast back home.

"Bring him to the barn, Tina," said Dallas sharply from inside the barn.

Tina shivered violently, then forced herself to sit straight, her chin high. Her cheeks stung where she'd been scratched by weeds earlier. "I won't bring Charger one step closer until you bring Phil and Blaze out here."

A pickup rattled past on the gravel road and Tina wanted to shout for it to stop.

Dallas stepped into the doorway. He'd changed his clothes and was wearing blue dress slacks and a blue and white plaid shirt. His hair was brushed neatly and he was smiling as if he was happy. "Howdy, Tina. Bring Charger here, please. The buyer will be here in a minute."

"Bring Phil and Blaze out here first." She clutched the reins tighter. "Phil! Phil, can you hear me?"

Dallas laughed. "You don't think he can answer you, do you? You can't see your hero or your horse until you bring Charger to me right to the stall I have cleaned for him. I don't want him dirty. Now, get him in here so I can unsaddle him and brush him down."

In her mind's eye she could see Phil tied and gagged, struggling desperately to get loose to help her.

Taking a deep breath she nudged Charger with her knees, and he walked forward.

"Good girl, Tina. Just keep coming." Dallas laughed gleefully. "I knew my plan would work! In just a short time I'll have all the money I need to get us away from here."

With a sinking heart she ducked her head and rode Charger into the dim interior of the barn. Sunlight filtered through wide cracks. Her hands were numb from gripping the reins. Oh, where was Phil? Where was Blaze?

From where she sat she could see the whole interior, and it was empty! No Blaze! No Phil!

Tina's head spun and she thought she would fall off Charger.

"Get down!"

Tina looked down at his upturned face and finally it focused. She swallowed hard. "Where's Phil?" she whispered hoarsely. "Where's Blaze?"

"Wouldn't you like to know?" He grinned and his brown eyes sparkled with mischief. "Get down and I'll tell you all about it."

Awkwardly she slipped off Charger's back and stumbled against Dallas. He caught her and steadied her. His touch sickened her and she tried to draw away.

"We're even now, Tina," he said softly. "Charger made us even. I don't hate you now. You're still the prettiest girl I know even with your hair in a rat's nest."

"Where's Phil?" she asked through a bone dry throat. Her eyes stung with hot tears. Dallas's aftershave lotion filled her nostrils, almost gagging her.

He pushed her away and she stumbled against the rotted wood of the stall. "Who cares? I want to take care of Charger right now. We'll talk about Phil later." He looked down at her, a strange look on his face. "We'll talk about you later, too."

She pressed her face against the stall and forced herself to stop trembling. She would not fall apart now! She would stay until she could get Phil and Blaze away from Dallas.

Dallas talked softly to Charger as he unsaddled him and brushed him. Tina listened, wondering how he could sound nice when he was so bad.

She shook her head and pursed her lips as she saw the halter Dallas had ready to slip on Charger. Dallas had thought of everything it seemed. How long had he been planning this?

Dallas stepped back from Charger, a proud look on his face. "Doesn't he look beautiful? I'd like him for myself. Maybe someday I can own a horse like this. Once I'm out of here,

I can find a way to make real money. Ma and I will live in style."

"Why lie to yourself, Dallas?" Tina asked tiredly.

His head snapped up. "What do you mean by that?"

"Dallas, you won't get far with this money from Charger. Jobs are hard to find in the city. Your mother won't be able to have a garden to help with food. She won't be happy." Tina threw up her hands. "Oh, what's the use? You don't even care! You only care about yourself!"

"I wouldn't talk if I were you, Miss Hotshot! You never cared about anybody but yourself."

She stared down at her boots. She had been that way once, but not now. At least, she hoped not. Jesus was teaching her to think of others.

He tapped her head and she looked up. "We don't have long to wait, Tina."

"Please take me to Phil and Blaze so I can go home."

"Sure. And give you time to tell someone that I have Charger here. You're staying until I have the money in my hand and Ma and me are on our way out."

"You . . . you mean I have to stay here the rest of the day?"

"Maybe. Who knows? I might decide to take you along. I could make up some story to tell Ma."

She shook her head helplessly. "No. No, Dallas. I want to go home right now."

He laughed. "I thought you were anxious to get Phil and Blaze away from me."

"I am! I do want them. Can't you at least tell me where they are?" She pressed her hands together in front of her and begged him with her eyes as well as her mouth.

He brushed a piece of straw off his pants. "That's for me to know and you to find out."

Her eyes flashed. "Oh, I wish I'd never met you! I wish that I hadn't gone to that picnic and talked to you."

"Telling me you were sixteen instead of thirteen."

She flushed. "Let me go home right now! I want out of here away from you, as far away as I can get!"

He reached for a white nylon rope hanging from a long nail. "Sit right down over there and I'll get you ready. I sure can't have you running outside when the buyer comes for Charger." He help up a large white hanky. "I'm ready for everything. This should keep you quiet enough."

Tears slipped down her suddenly pale cheeks as he reached for her.

THIRTEEN

A Wild Ride

"I've really got you this time," said Dallas with a chuckle.

She backed away from him, her eyes on the rope in his hands.

"Did you really think I had Phil and Blaze? I don't. I knew Phil was going to be gone for the day. Bridget told me." He looked down at her in triumph. "She said Blaze would be gone too. I found a way to use that valuable information, don't you think?"

Anger rushed through her and she leaped against him, catching him off guard and he stumbled backward enough so that she could get around him. In a flash she clambered up the ladder to the haymow, her heart racing.

"You won't get away from me, Tina!" He started up behind her, then stopped at the sound of a horn honking outside.

Tina tripped and sprawled across the dusty floor, choking and sneezing.

"You're too late to save Charger, Tina," said Dallas firmly. "The buyer is here and he sure won't let this opportunity slip through his fingers. You're outnumbered, smarty. I won!" He laughed. "This buyer knows he's buying a stolen horse and he doesn't care."

Tina peeked through a crack in the floor and watched Dallas walk out of the barn just as the horn honked again. Oh, what could she do! She could not let the man buy Charger!

Cautiously she walked across the mow floor and peeked out the crack beside the window. A pickup with a tan and brown horse trailer stood in the driveway. As Dallas stepped out of the barn a man climbed from the pickup. She had never seen the tall, broad-shouldered man before. He ignored Dallas's outstretched hand.

"Show me this gelding, then we'll talk hard cash," he said in a gruff voice. "I know it's good stock, coming from Lambert's, but I want to see him."

"He's right in here."

"Lead him out. I want a look at him in sunlight." The man shoved back his wide-brimmed hat and Tina saw his bushy mustache and his dark hair.

Tina waited anxiously, hardly daring to breath. What if Dallas told the man she was in the haymow? He would never let her go.

She heard Dallas talking gently to Charger as he led him from the barn. How would they ever load him in the trailer? He wasn't used to a horse trailer yet. Had Dallas thought about that?

Dallas walked Charger around and around as the man studied him with care. Finally he instructed Dallas to tie the lead rope to the trailer and they'd get the money taken care of. She saw Dallas look up at the mow, then quickly away. Was he worried she'd show herself?

Charger pranced nervously while Dallas and the man walked to the front of the pickup to talk. Tina heard them disagree over the price and she saw the set look on Dallas's face. He would not let the man talk him down.

Carefully Tina walked to the ladder and climbed down, her heart in her mouth. Would they stop arguing enough to hear the noise her boots made on the wooden ladder? She waited, poised for flight. She could hear their voices getting angrier.

She ran to the back of the barn and out the door into the bright sunlight. She carefully walked around the barn, climbed through a barbed wire fence, then stopped at the corner closest to Charger. Could she ride Charger back to the ranch bareback with just a halter? Would he throw her right at Dallas's feet?

Carefully she peeked around the corner, her breath caught in her throat. Could she reach Charger before they could stop her?

The man angrily agreed to Dallas's price.

He pulled out his wallet and started counting out the bills in Dallas's outstretched hand. Now was her chance! Dallas would never drop money to grab her.

In a flash she dashed to the horse trailer. With one motion she jerked the slipknot lose and swung onto Charger's back, scrambling to get seated before he bolted.

"What in the world!" cried the man in astonishment.

"Tina!" screamed Dallas, lunging toward Tina and Charger.

Charger leaped with a snort and Tina clung desperately to the rope and Charger's mane. She pressed her knees tightly against the gelding's sides and leaned forward. She felt Dallas's hands brush her leg before Charger bolted down the driveway into the open pasture. Wind whipped her already tangled hair. Pounding hooves drummed in her head, drowning out the shouting she'd left behind.

Would Charger instinctively head home? What would happen if he suddenly came upon a fence?

Perspiration trickled down her body, wetting her blouse only to have the wind whip it dry. Her legs ached from holding them tight against Charger. She knew they were on Farenholz property. Would Jim Bridger bark a warning to Codge? Maybe she could stop Charger and run to Codge for help.

A jackrabbit leaped high, startling Charger.

He veered right and Tina shouted whoa, but he didn't obey. Charger was headed toward Tanner Hill instead of home! She jerked on the lead rope but Charger fought against the tug and would not be turned.

Silently, urgently Tina cried out for protection and help from her heavenly Father. He had helped her to get away from Dallas. He would continue to help her until she was safely home! The thought comforted her and she tried to relax against Charger and ride out his run. He would tire soon and stop. He had to!

He ran along a barbed wire fence, found a part down and leaped over it, almost toppling Tina off. Maybe she should've just let herself fall the way she'd trained herself to fall off Blaze in a roll, then land on her feet. But she must stay with Charger and get him home again. Dad had a buyer for him already, and Dad hated to go back on his word to anyone. She had to stay on Charger!

He splashed through a stream, wetting her legs. Oh, she'd like a tall glass of ice water! Or a bath in cool water!

"Whoa, Charger!" she cried again, tugging on the lead rope. "Whoa!" Had he slowed just a little? Her heart leaped, then dropped dismally. He was not stopping. She thought she would slide off over his head as he ran downhill.

Did Hawk know yet that Charger was gone?

Would he immediately think she was up to something bad?

Where was Blaze? Had he been stolen by someone or had Phil taken him for the day for some reason?

Charger stumbled and Tina flew up, then landed awkwardly. Charger reared, then landed with a thud. Tina sailed over his neck without a chance to position her fall. She landed face down, the tall weeds padding her fall a little. Her head spun and she couldn't move.

Finally she pushed herself painfully up and sat in the tall grass, the sun hot against her. A grasshopper landed on her leg, and hopped away. A bee buzzed around her head. Tears slipped down her cheeks, stinging the scratches. Where was Charger? How would she catch him now?

Painfully she stood up, her hands pressed against her lower back. She blinked away her tears as she looked for Charger. Finally she spotted him in the distance. She had to catch him! She had to take him home to Dad and Hawk!

Slowly, awkwardly, she walked toward Charger. Finally the pain left her body and she could walk a little better.

A plane flew overhead, shattering the stillness. She looked up, shielding her eyes against the sun. It was Bob Grover's plane. Maybe he would see her and call her house and ask why she was on foot so far away from home.

"Charger!" she called, cupping her hands around her mouth. She called again and again until her parched throat couldn't take it. At least Charger had stopped running and was grazing.

Finally she drew close enough that he raised his head, knowing she was there. Her legs felt too heavy to move but she had to go on.

"Easy, Charger," she said softly, her hand out to him. "I want to take you home where you can have a drink of water and some grain. Wouldn't you like that?"

He tossed his head and ran a few steps away, then stopped, his nose in the tall grass.

Tina walked wide around him and came up on him from his side where his lead rope dragged the ground.

Slowly, slowly she walked toward Charger, her hand reaching for the halter strap or lead rope. Her fingers brushed against the rope and Charger leaped away.

With a sob Tina sank to the ground, covering her face with her hands. Why keep trying? She couldn't catch Charger. He didn't want to be caught.

Finally the tears stopped and she brushed her eyes dry and rubbed her nose with the back of her hand. She could not quit! She would never quit! She remembered Mary telling her that she was not alone, was never alone.

"God is always with you to help you, Tina," Mary had said often. "Just take his help and his strength."

Tina rubbed her hands down her jeans as she stood up. She wrapped her arms around herself and closed her eyes, talking quietly to her heavenly Father.

Unusual strength flowed through her and she actually was able to smile. "Thank you, Father. Thank you that you are going to help me catch Charger."

By the time she caught up with him again her stomach was cramped and growling with hunger. Soon it would be supper time. What had Mary done when she hadn't been home for lunch?

"Charger, whoa, boy. I'm going to catch you. I'm going to lead you home. Easy, big fellow. You don't have to be afraid of me. I'm your friend."

Her hand closed around the halter strap and she leaned her head weakly against Charger. Tears slipped down her cheeks, tears of joy and thanksgiving.

"We're going home, Charger. We're going home right now." She held the halter strap with her right hand and looped the lead rope through her left hand.

"Let's go, boy." She tugged and he walked obediently beside her.

FOURTEEN

Bridget Hawksley

The sun was almost hidden behind the tall hill across the road from the house as Tina walked into the ranch yard with Charger.

"Tina!" cried Bridget in surprise.

Tina looked at her in a daze.

"Daddy! Daddy, Tina has Charger!" shouted Bridget in the direction of the bunkhouse. Then she turned back to Tina. "I knew you'd taken him! I knew you had to get even with Daddy."

Tina frowned and slowly shook her head. "No," she whispered through cracked lips. "No."

"You look awful! I bet he bucked you off. You're not the rider you thought you were, are you?"

Before she could answer Hawk ran up, then stopped short, his dark eyes wide in surprise.

"What happened to you, little girl?" He turned to his daughter. "Get Steve now! Run! Run, Bridget, and get Steve!"

Bridget hesitated, then turned and raced toward the ranch house. She looked back at Tina once, then ran on, dust puffing up around her.

"I'll take Charger now," said Hawk gently. "You look like a good stiff breeze would blow you over."

She opened her mouth to speak, but no words came out. Hawk seemed to be floating. She felt his hand on her fingers as he pried her loose from the halter strap. Her legs buckled and she would've fallen but he caught her, his strong arm around her slender waist.

"What happened to Tina?"

She heard Phil's voice and tears slipped down her cheeks. "Phil? Is it really you?" With a sob she held her hands out to him and he pulled her into his arms, holding her.

"What happened to you, Tina?" he asked against her hair. "You look like you've been in a fight."

Suddenly Steve and Mary were there and Steve lifted her in his arms and carried her to the house, his face set. She heard Bridget ask Phil what he thought happened, but she couldn't hear Phil's answer. Oh, Phil was safe! Was Blaze?

She lifted her head off Steve's chest. "Blaze. Is Blaze all right?" she whispered hoarsely.

"Don't talk," snapped Steve.

She clutched at his shirt. "Daddy, is Blaze home?"

He stopped and frowned down at her. "I don't know and right now I don't care. I want to take you in the house and see if you're hurt."

"Blaze," she whimpered, struggling.

"I'll check on Blaze for you," said Mary as she opened the back door. "I'll be right back."

Steve gently laid her on the couch and knelt beside her. "Will you be all right while I find water and a washcloth?"

She nodded, listening for Mary to come back. The mantel clock chimed six. Tina heard running water, then the door opened and closed. She lifted her head, her eyes boring into Mary as she walked across the room.

Mary knelt beside Tina and patted her arm. "Blaze is in his stall right where he should be. Bridget said he's been there all day."

"No! He was gone!" She tried to push herself up but she was too weak and tired.

"Why does it matter, honey?" asked Mary softly. "You lie back and let us clean you up to see just how bad the cuts on your face are."

Tina carefully touched her face. "Is it bloody?"

"Yes. You look as if you've been dragged around the pasture on your face." Mary squeezed her hand and smiled. "I'm glad you're home and that you're safe. We were ready to send out a search party. One of the men said you'd gone to the pines to meet Phil."

Steve stood over her beside Mary. "But Phil said he hadn't left such a message. He knew he was going to be gone all day to town. He said he told Slim to tell you."

"Daddy, are you mad about Charger? Is he all right? Did he get hurt?"

"I'll get a report from Hawk on Charger when we've finished with you." He carefully washed her forehead, then her cheeks. "We have some talking to do, little girl. You were forbidden to take Charger for a ride, or even out of his corral."

"I know," she whispered, then before she could stop herself, she burst into wild sobbing. She felt Steve's arms around her, pulling her against his wide chest. She wrapped her arms around his waist and sobbed against his shirt. The smell and feel of him soothed her until finally she was able to gulp back the tears.

"I think Tina should go right in and soak in the tub," said Mary firmly. "After a warm bath and clean clothes, she'll be able to tell us what happened."

"You're right, Mary." Steve held Tina away from him and looked down into her face. "You go with Mary. I'll talk to Hawk and come in later after your bath."

Tina could only nod.

"Come on, honey," said Mary, tugging Tina's hand. "I'll fill the tub while you undress."

In the bathroom Tina looked in the mirror and cried out in horror. Was she that wild-looking girl?

"Don't let it scare you, Tina," said Mary with a laugh. "Once you get the blood off and your hair in order, you won't look so bad."

The water stung her scratches as she slipped down in the warm water. Once she was under, she never wanted to leave. Bubbles that smelled like strawberries floated around and over her. Mary carefully washed her hair, using plenty of cream rinse to take out the tangles.

"None of the scratches are deep, Tina," said Mary as she laid out a towel. "Your face should be healed in a few days. A couple on your arms might take a while longer."

She felt more like herself once she was dressed in jeans and a light green cotton tee shirt and her hair hung over her shoulders in two long braids.

With a deep breath she pulled the threatening notes out of her desk drawer. She had a lot to tell Dad and Mary.

Tina stopped in surprise in the front room. Bridget stood beside the piano, her hands clasped together tightly, a worried frown on her face. "What do you want?" asked Tina sharply. "Are you ready to tell Dallas a few more family secrets?"

"What secrets? He's been lying to you. I only told him things about me and the ranch." She was dressed in blue shorts and a light blue suntop. Her red hair capped her head attractively. She needed Charger to buck her off into the tall weeds and briers!

"Bridget, what did you do with Blaze?"

She backed away, her eyes full of fear. "Who says I did anything?"

Tina walked slowly toward her, her hands at her sides. "Bridget, I know Blaze was gone. You were the one to take him so Dallas could force me to steal Charger for him."

"What?" she shrieked, her hand at her throat. "I didn't know! I honestly didn't know!"

"I don't believe you. I think you knew what he was planning and I think you helped him."

Bridget shook her head helplessly, her hands out to Tina. "No! I wouldn't do that! I thought he wanted to get even with you for what you did to him before I came."

"And what was that?" Tina's eyes narrowed and she waited impatiently for the answer.

"He said you dropped him for Phil. He said you broke his heart!"

"And you believed him! You *are* stupid, Bridget! I'll tell you why he wanted to get even." Angrily she told the story. She watched

Bridget's face turn white and she had to hold the back of Steve's chair for support.

"I didn't know," she whispered.

"Now you know." Tina stepped around Steve's chair beside Bridget. "Did you take Blaze?"

She nodded helplessly. "He said that would make you really mad. He said it would help both of us pay you back." She licked her lips. "I am sorry, Tina. I really am."

"Did you hurt Blaze?"

"No. I rode around, then tied him up down by the pond. I put him into his stall a while ago. I . . . I won't touch him again. I promise!"

"See that you don't."

"Will you tell Daddy? Will he be fired?"

Tina wanted to tell her that that's exactly what would happen, but she stopped. God wanted her to forgive Bridget. And it wouldn't be right to punish Hawk for something his daughter did. Finally Tina sighed and shook her head. "I will tell Hawk what you did, but I'll tell him that you're sorry and that I forgave you. Dad won't fire Hawk. He needs him and he likes him."

"Thank you, Tina," whispered Bridget. She turned and rushed from the room out the front door.

Tina turned at a sound behind her. Steve and Mary stood there.

"We heard," said Steve gruffly, tears sparkling in his eyes. "But now we want to hear it all, every last detail."

"And don't leave anything out," said Mary. "This time something is going to be done about Dallas Tromley."

Tina sank down on Steve's chair and waited until Mary and Steve were seated side by side on the couch. Taking a deep breath, she started the story of her adventure.

FIFTEEN

Phil

Tina pressed her face against Blaze's neck. He nickered softly. She had wanted to rush right out to him after she'd told Dad and Mary about the threatening notes and Dallas's plan, but Mary had insisted that she eat something first. Dad had said he'd eat when he got back from talking to Mrs. Tromley. Tina asked him to bring back her saddle and bridle and in a grim voice he said he would.

"I'm glad you're safe, Blaze," she said softly. "I couldn't live without you."

"I'm glad *you're* safe, Tina."

She turned with a happy smile as Phil walked up to her. "Hi." She knew her smile spread from ear to ear.

"I know you've been telling what happened, but I want to hear it, please. I don't think I can sleep until I know what went on and that you're really all right."

She patted Blaze one last time, then walked

with Phil to a bale of hay and sat with him.

He caught her hand and held it in a tight grip and she returned the pressure. She was safe! Phil was beside her and not tied up in Dallas's barn!

In a low voice she told Phil all that had happened. He interrupted her from time to time with a sympathetic word or angry exclamation. She told him how God had helped her to forgive Bridget for her part in it and he said it would be a real miracle if he could forgive Bridget. She knew how he felt because she was struggling with forgiving Dallas. He did not deserve to be forgiven! She had every right to hate him and be bitter toward him and hold a grudge against him. But Mary had shown her in the Bible where Jesus said to forgive and it didn't say a word about certain conditions. Mary had said forgiveness was important to her, that if she held the anger inside she would only hurt herself.

She shared with Phil how God had given her the strength to catch Charger and walk home with him. How thankful she was!

"And to think I was safe in Braden with Smokey!" Phil pressed his lips tightly together and a frown wrinkled his forehead.

Tina laughed up at him. "Hey! I'm glad you were. I sure didn't want you tied up somewhere for a coyote to eat you or something."

His face relaxed into a grin. "I see what you mean. I'll be glad when we're in school next week. You won't have time to get into trouble."

"I'll be glad of that! I've had enough excitement to last me a long, long time."

"What do you think Steve will do to Dallas?" asked Phil thoughtfully. "I know how much he likes and respects Mrs. Tromley."

"Dallas is all she has. Her husband walked out on them when Dallas was eleven. He's still very bitter. He wants to make things easier for his mother."

"Hey!" Phil leaped to his feet and stood staring down at her, his hands on his hips. "Do you feel sorry for that creep?"

She stood up and touched Phil's arm. "No. Well, maybe just a little. I know God could help him if he'd let him."

"Dallas could help his mother in the ordinary way by working and helping her. He doesn't have to be on the lookout for get-rich-quick schemes."

"I know. Maybe after Dad's done talking to him, he'll get his head on straight."

Just then Hawk stepped into the barn, asking Tina if he could talk to her alone.

Phil looked at her, his brow raised questioningly. She nodded and he walked out, saying he'd wait for her beside the corral fence.

Tina saw the hesitation on Hawk's face as he rolled his wide-brimmed hat in his hands.

"Bridget told me," he said barely above a whisper. "I'm sorry, little girl. I'm sorry she hurt you. She's being punished. She won't do it again."

"Did she tell you that she said she was sorry?"

He nodded.

"And that I forgave her?"

He nodded again. "Steve said he didn't want me leaving. I sure would if you said the word."

She pushed her hands into her jeans pockets and shook her head. "I don't want you to leave. You're too good with horses." She grinned and shrugged. "Besides, I like you."

"Steve said you rode Charger bareback with only a halter."

She shrugged again. "He bucked me off."

"I think you should be helping me train the horses along with Phil. You'd be just about the best person I can think of to work with me." He clamped his hat on his head and stood with his hands lightly on his hips. "What do you say?"

She tipped her head and looked up at him. "I'd like that. I'll work with you all I can. But with school starting, I won't have much time."

Hawk turned his head. "I hear your dad driving in. I know you want to talk to him, so I'll say good night. See you in the morning."

She held out her hand and he took it in a firm handshake. "See you in the morning, Hawk."

"Tina, Steve's back," said Phil from the doorway, his voice low with excitement.

In a few minutes, Tina's saddle was in place in the tack room and she stood beside the corral with Steve and Phil. Before Steve said anything Mary hurried from the house. It would be dark soon. Tina moved closer to Phil and he caught her hand and held it.

Steve draped his arm around Mary's shoulder. "I didn't have to say much to Mrs. Tromley. She found Tina's saddle in the barn and forced Dallas to tell her what had happened. She said she's taking Dallas away from here. She has a brother in New Mexico who wants them with him. He'll help her with Dallas."

"What about the ranch? Can she sell it?" asked Mary anxiously. "I know she needs the money she has tied up in it."

"Believe it or not Codge is going to buy the place. She called him about it and he said his nephew and family are moving west and want a place. He's going to fix it up for them." Steve caught Tina's free hand and squeezed. "You won't have to worry about Dallas Tromley again, Tina."

"Good!" She blinked back tears. "I hope he can be helped."

"He will be," said Mary. "He has prayers going up for him."

"It's getting dark out here," said Steve. "Let's go in. I'm hungry. Anything to eat?"

"Plenty," said Mary happily. "I'll warm it up right away."

"Dad, I'm going to stay out just a little longer," said Tina. "I want to talk to Phil a while."

"Don't stay out too long or I'll come looking for you," said Steve, tugging a braid. "I mean it. You're important to me, little girl. I love you."

"I love you, Daddy. I won't stay out long. I promise." She stood with Phil as her dad and Mary walked to the house.

"I'm glad you didn't go in," said Phil softly. "I wanted to tell you something."

"Let me talk first, okay?" She turned to him and he caught both hands in his. "Phil, I'm sorry for being jealous of you and Bridget. If you like her better, I'll try not to pull out her hair or anything else childish."

"Tina, Tina. I don't like Bridget better than you. I thought you knew that."

"But you spent so much time with her! Every time I turned around you were with her!"

"Steve asked me to make her feel welcome. That's all I was doing." He grinned, "It makes me feel kind of good to know that you were jealous."

She tugged free. "It didn't make me feel good! I hated it!" She turned to go to the house but he caught her arm.

"Wait."

"Why?"

He hesitated, his grip tightening. "I love you."

She stood perfectly still, her heart pounding loud enough for him to hear. "You do?"

"Yes."

She touched his cheek. "I love you."

He bent down and his lips touched hers. She returned his kiss, then said good night.

"See you in the morning, Phil."

"First thing," he said with a grin.

Tina ran to the house, her heart singing.